WITHDRAWN

Iva-Marie Palmer

GABBY GARCIA'S
ULTIMATE PLAYBOOK

SIDELINED

Illustrations by Marta Kissi

KATHERINE TEGEN BOOKS
An Imprint of HarperCollins Publishers

Katherine Tegen Books is an imprint of HarperCollins Publishers.

Gabby Garcia's Ultimate Playbook #3: Sidelined

ISBN 978-0-06-239186-5

Typography by Katie Fitch
19 20 21 22 23 PC/LSCH 10 9 8 7 6 5 4 3 2 1
❖
First Edition

To you, the reader:
I cheer for you

AUGUST 17 PLAYBOOK!

I'm going to Seattle!

It's pretty cool, because we never go **ANYWHERE**. Well, we do, and we have, but the last few years Louie has been so busy at work, and Dad has had all these projects, and blah blah blah that we only really went to see my grandma in Florida. (Just over the border so it might as well still be Georgia.)

But in just a few short hours, I'm going **MILES** across the **COUNTRY**! On a plane! I already called the window seat! Plus, we have tickets to a Mariners game! Also, even though I never thought about it before, Seattle sounds interesting! For one, what is a **SPACE NEEDLE**? It sounds both high-tech and dangerous! There are also **KILLER WHALES** in Puget Sound, and we don't have those here, that's for sure. Dad and Louie signed up for a cheese-making workshop at Pike Place Market. (Making a dairy product seems like a lot of work to me, but grown-ups are weird.) While they're cheesing it up, I'm going to find the market's gum wall, where people stick their chewed gum. It sounds both gross and photo-worthy!

WHERE SHOULD I LEAVE MY USED GUM?

DON'T CHEW-SE THIS SPOT!

SEATTLE GUM WALL

VS

STICK TO APPROVED PLACES!

So . . .

My **GOAL**: To come back to Peach Tree with the **BEST** "what I did on my summer vacation" story.

My **STRATEGY: TAKE SEATTLE BY STORM**! I have a guidebook from the Peach Tree Public Library and a list of places to make my mark (and stick my gum).

I'm really in the zone when it comes to, well, being me. Or my best possible me. When I first started Piper Bell, I had to learn what really mattered to me (**PLAYING** baseball more than always **WINNING** at it), and this summer, I realized some things about how to be a good friend when Diego, my forever bestie, came back from Costa Rica.

Now, with all that working for me, I figure my eighth-grade year can be **REALLY AMAZING**. Finally, I know **EXACTLY** what I'm doing . . .

Well.

Maybe I only **SEEM** like I know what I'm doing. I think sometimes my insides don't match my outsides. It's a lot like baseball. On the mound, I might seem in control at all times. I'll be throwing strikes until a thought creeps in: What if I screw up and let the next batter get a home run and the game turns around? What if that was the last good fastball I'll ever throw?

I wonder if it happens to every player. Or maybe to **EVERYONE**, even in regular things. What if we're all trying to manage insides that don't always match our outsides?

Maybe it's okay to pretend you have a handle on things on the outside, as long as you know that everyone has inside stuff like yours.

Whew. I guess I'm saying I'm glad you're here, Playbook, so I have a place to strategize the inside stuff. For now, it's time to go on vacation. We deserve a break.

AUGUST 24
THE RECAP

Major league error alert! I will never **EVER EVER EVER** say I'm going to take anything by storm again.

This time, I ended up **ALL WET**.

I'm never setting foot in Seattle again. (This is going to be hard when I'm a major league pitcher, but I think I will forfeit those games because I plan to hold this grudge forever.) First of all, if it's not raining—and it rains **ALL THE TIME**—Seattle is gray. It shouldn't be allowed to say it has summer because gray is **NOT** the official color of summer. Summer is **GREEN**. And **BLUE**. And **RAINBOWS**. (Ugh, fine, so rainbows require rain, but they also require sun. Which doesn't exist in Seattle!)

If the gray wasn't bad enough, I had to share a hotel room with Peter. The room was beautiful and clean for two seconds, and then Peter took off his shoes and socks, and his **FOOT SMELL** fouled up the air so much even the cute mini bottles of shampoo couldn't make me feel better. As I sat at the window, trying to admire the **GRAYNESS**, he started playing his video game and narrating every move he made, adding noise pollution to his foot stench.

There were **OKAY** things. At the Space Needle, you can see for miles and, from that standpoint, the view of the water and the trees are better than okay. And the air is exactly what fresh air is supposed to be like, all refreshing and like minty gum for your brain. I breathed so much of it the first day, I fell right asleep and had dreams of stepping out of the Space Needle onto a cloud and playing baseball in the sky on a team of my favorite players (plus, weirdly, Amelia Earhart and the mayor of Atlanta and a dog in a spacesuit) with miles of water beneath me.

But Seattle was out to get me. It had tricked me with sweet dreams and nice views. Because on the second day of the trip, at the Mariners game, I tripped.

I tripped on a hot dog.

That someone had dropped between the aisles of seats. WHO DROPS A HOT DOG?

THE ONLY OCCASIONS WHEN IT'S OKAY TO ABANDON A HOT DOG

- If you're a vegetarian (but maybe see if you can find a hot dog lover to hand it to)

- If someone has put pizza toppings on it (you would think this would make a hot dog better but it is a bad combination)

- If you are really full and have no room in your

stomach to give it a good home (but again, see if
you can find your hot dog that home in someone
else's stomach)

- According to people in Chicago, if it has ketchup
  on it

I went flying face forward into the next concrete step
and my left arm came down hard. And **SNAP**! Or **CRACK**!
One of those. I can't remember the sound because **IT HURT
SO MUCH**.

THE
HOT DOG
THAT'S TO
BLAME

I stood up too fast even though people had gotten up from their seats to see if I was okay. When I was on my feet and looking down at the hot dog I'd fallen over, it felt like my insides were swimming on my outsides and suddenly I threw up—right on my favorite red high-tops.

I know pitchers are sometimes called hurlers and maybe that's a little funny but **I WAS NOT** laughing.

We had to leave the game to get my arm set. My fracture was only partial (and on my non-pitching left arm, thank goodness), but I'd still need a cast for four to six weeks! The Seattle doctors offered me a billion color options for my cast and I was so mad at their city I said, "It doesn't matter," because they couldn't butter me up with a designer cast.

Louie bought me a pair of really boring black sneakers because Seattle didn't have red high-tops. At Pike Place Market, the sun actually came out and I realized I'd lost my sunglasses when they'd **FLOWN OFF MY HEAD** when **I TRIPPED ON A HOT DOG**. I was so miserable I didn't get anything to eat, so when we took a boat ride on Puget Sound I got seasick and had to hang out below deck. Peter saw three whales while I tried not to barf again.

Instead of me taking Seattle by storm, Seattle had taken me by drizzle. (Drizzle is the worst form of precipitation

because it can't make up its mind. Be a downpour! Or be a gentle mist! A drizzle is just uncomfortable.)

If I was worried about my insides matching my outsides, in Seattle, my insides matched **EVERYTHING OUTSIDE**. Gloomy weather went perfectly with **GLOOMY ME**.

One week and one cast later, I'm back, two nights before school starts, with an itchy and sweaty arm, pretending to be sick so I don't have to show my friends my dumb cast—it ended up being **NEON ORANGE**. I'll never tell a doctor "it doesn't matter" again. I look like I punched a traffic cone. Also, because I normally use my left hand to write, I can barely even scribble this! I'm holding the pencil in my right like a strange bird Diego probably loves. It stinks! Basically, I am mad at everything.

When I said we deserved a break, Playbook, this wasn't what I had in mind.

Gabby Garcia

↳ THE CURRENT STATE OF MY SIGNATURE...

Good night.

THE CHARMING DISARMING

Goal: Not let my bum arm hog the spotlight on the first day of school

Action: Keep it under wraps

Post-Day Analysis:
August 26

I woke up yesterday morning feeling **SO NOT READY** to go back to school. I wanted the first day of eighth grade to be **PERFECT** and a broken arm was not part of the plan.

My room was my bullpen, but for emotions and plans instead of pitches. I needed to get into the right mental state.

I thought about talking to my friends, but they'd be concerned and supportive because they'd feel sorry for me. The last thing I needed was to be guest of honor at a pity party.

What I **WANTED**, the emotional bullpen helped me figured out, was a way to walk into school like someone
who—after a few false starts when I was trying too hard
to have an MVP Summer—had had a great summer. Having a cast was like proof I hadn't. Was there any bright
side to a broken arm? (Ha, my orange cast has nothing but
bright sides.)

Also, what about running for class president? If everyone heard I tripped on a hot dog, no one would see me as
a take-charge kind of person.

Staring at the ceiling, I figured something out: it

wouldn't be baseball season until spring. No one **HAD** to see my arm.

I would hide the broken arm! At least for the first few days, just till I had eighth grade figured out. Simple!

I'd hide my cast with clothing!

SO TODAY'S FIRST-DAY OUTFIT INCLUDED THE FOLLOWING:

DAD'S BOWLER HAT

FLOWY SCARF (LOUIE'S)

PIPER BELL JACKET

ROLLED SCHOOL PANTS

NOTHING TO SEE HERE, FOLKS!

HIGH-TOPS

- Long-sleeved shirt

- Piper Bell jacket

- Flowy scarf (Louie's)

- Piper Bell uniform pants

- Red high-tops

- Fun hat! To draw the eye **UP** and **AWAY** from my arm.

There were a few flaws to my disguise. One: the end of August is **HOT**. And, two: my arm wasn't very **BENDY** so I had to wear the jacket draped over my shoulder and kind of balance it there.

12

"Haha," Peter said as he walked out the door this morning in his soccer jersey and shorts. "You look like someone collecting money for a charity, and you're the charity."

His insults were getting better. But also, **MEAN**!

I didn't **LOVE** the outfit. But it was better than my **BUMMER SUMMER** story. I would need to balance my weird "look" by being really happy about **EVERYTHING**. When beaming bright like the sun, no one can look right at you. Or your arm.

Unfortunately, I'd failed to plan for a few other **FIRST-DAY FACTORS**:

Opening a locker. I may pitch with my right hand, but I do a lot of little stuff (holding a pen, locker-dial turning) with my left. Putting in my combo right-handed took forever.

Double high fives! Maybe they were a first-day thing but all the eighth graders had decided on the two-handed high five as a way to say "welcome back!" I left a lot of people hanging.

Sudden movements. Like when I heard Katy call my name in the hall and I turned around and my jacket started to slide down my bad arm. I scooped it back onto my shoulder before anyone noticed anything.

"Gabby! Happy new school year!" she said, bounding into place at my locker. I was so happy to see her, I wanted to hug her, but that would have definitely tipped her off to my arm. "Do you feel better?"

I looked at her with alarm in my eyes.

"SHH!" I'd forgotten I'd told her I was sick.

"What is it? What's with the scarf? You look like a real estate agent. But I like it. It's . . . interesting. Or . . . do you have a chill? It's eighty-six degrees outside! If you're sick . . ."

I wiped a bead of sweat from my eyebrow and enviously eyeballed Katy's short-sleeved T-shirt and skirt, which was printed with brightly colored tropical fruit.

I leaned in close to Katy like I was sharing exclusive spy secrets. "I broke my arm." I had to tell her. Hiding facts from my friend was too strange.

"What? Why? How?" She took a closer look. "Whew, it's not your pitching arm."

"I know, right? I'm so glad it's not my right," I said and laughed at my joke. My funny bone wasn't broken, after all.

"Why are you hiding it?" Katy said. "People are going to figure it out eventually."

Katy had said she would run for class president, too. So a little part of me wondered if she thought her opponent being down for the count with a broken arm might help her chances. Not that she wanted me hurt, but sometimes

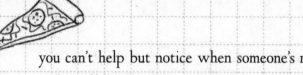

you can't help but notice when someone's not game-ready and you'll have an advantage. Competitors are like that.

"Where do we need to go to sign up for the election?" I asked, avoiding her question and trying to find out what her plans were. Also, I really needed to get out of the hot, sweaty hallway, and the classrooms had AC.

She shook her head. "I decided not to do it. I don't think I can handle adding one more hyphen to my title." Katy was a singer-dancer-songwriter and Peach Tree's biggest celebrity. "I'm heading up talent squad this year, plus I might do some workshops with a youth group and my mom's all concerned it will be"—she made her voice grown-uppy—"time-consuming."

I laughed at her impression of her mom but also felt a little zing in my heart: my chances to get elected had gone up. Katy could have won in a heartbeat, or at least a few heartbeats. Then she asked, "Now tell me why you have to hide your arm." She was such a good friend that I felt the slightest bit guilty for being glad about her not running for president.

"If you have to know, I can't tell anyone about my arm because . . ." I looked around like we were spies trading secrets in a parking garage. ". . . how it happened is incredibly embarrassing."

"My cousin Eddie once got part of his arm stuck in a Pringles can, so how could yours be worse?"

So I told her. The whole hot dog fiasco.

And, she doubled over in laughter.

"That is **WAY** worse than a Pringles-jar arm!" She slung her arm gently over my shoulders and shook her head at me. "But also, you should **OWN** that story. You can't make that stuff up! I mean, a hot dog?? I don't know **ANYONE** who has ever tripped over a hot dog." She wiped laugh-tears from her eyes, and as I replayed the moment in my head, I realized it **WAS** pretty funny.

"*You* get it, but I guess I wanted to start eighth grade in the easiest way possible. Plus, if I decide to run for president, I need to seem like I'm in control and in charge." It was true, and I gingerly tried to fling the scarf back over my neck to emphasize the point, knocking off my hat and dropping my books as I did so.

"Just saying, wearing forty layers of clothing is maybe not the way to do that," Katy said as she crouched to hand me my geometry workbook.

"People might think it's a look."

"Okay, Gabby Girl, you do you," Katy said. "But I don't think you need to be *this* you."

Weirdly, though, people did think my layers were a look. Or, at least the new kids in the sixth grade seemed to, as they eyeballed me like maybe I knew something they didn't. And so I smiled brightly and felt like my campaign was underway already! Maybe I'd start a new fashion trend during my run for class president, like Hillary Clinton had with pantsuits.

By *seeming* to have things under control, it was like I already did. When I got to lunch period, I was walking on air. If I got this school year started on an upbeat note, then when I did reveal the cast, it would be no big deal because my campaign would be more important.

I found a seat at the cafeteria, which at Piper Bell is called the café. I was supposed to be sitting with Johnny. It was the first time I'd seen him since I went to Seattle. He is maybe my boyfriend, or at least definitely a boy who is more than a friend. We talk and text pretty often and hold hands and sometimes I think about his green eyes for no apparent reason, other than they're really nice to look at.

"Hi," he said, walking up his usual tie, but a new one in light green. It made his green eyes look even greener. So basically, I'd never stop thinking about them.

I smiled and tried to maneuver my PB&J out of my lunch sack with one hand and take the tiniest nibble so the jacket wouldn't slide off my shoulder. I should have given my outfit a night-before test run.

VOTE GABBY

"Your outfit is . . . unique. It has a lot of . . . pieces. Are you cold?" Johnny said, looking extremely concerned. I realized I could tell Johnny. If I'd told Katy, I **HAD** to tell my maybe-boyfriend, and also—what if he wrote something super sweet on my cast?

Yep, I had to tell him. I was about to when Devon DeWitt and Mario Salamida plopped down at our table. They're on the Penguins baseball team with me, and the two members of the team I'm closest with.

Devon looked at me for two seconds, got her glinty-eyed look, and said, "Gabby, you broke your arm," in her state-all-the-facts-very-clearly way. Devon is a pitcher, too, and she doesn't miss anything. Also, like her fastball, she's very direct.

"No, I didn't." I didn't want to lie but her observation came at me so fast, I blurted it out.

She pointed. "Why would you be wearing your jacket like that? Without your arm inside it?"

If Devon weren't a pitcher, she could head up some kind of intimidating government agency that ultimately changes the world for the better even though at first glance it would be hard to tell what side she was on.

"I thought it was a look," Mario said. Mario used to be my archrival because when we played Little League against each other, he never could get a hit off me and he wasn't a very good sportsperson about it. He's working on it, same as I'm working on handling not winning. (See? I still have trouble saying **LOSING**!) Now that we're friends, though, he's a big softie. "I like it. There's a lot going on, but it works."

"I did, too," Johnny said. "Like it. In a confused way. Because your normal look is good, too." He blushed like he'd said the wrong thing, but I thanked him as my heart thudded around and he looked relieved.

Devon blinked at Mario, then at Johnny. She does that a lot. Blink. Usually when she's thinking, or trying to get you to see you're off base about something. "It's clear she has a broken arm." She narrowed her eyes at me. "But why are you hiding it?"

She was right. I can say it as I write this: the Charming Disarming wasn't a great play, or a play at all. It was a cover-up, or a denial. Like a runner standing on first base even after the ump calls them out. They're still out, and I would have a cast for at least a month. When will I get better at accepting that things can't always go the way I see them going in my head?

"I guess I wanted a great start to eighth great, I mean,

grade!" I looked at Johnny, hoping he wasn't mad that I hadn't told him.

He smiled in a way that said he knew I had my reasons, and asked, "Did it hurt?"

"It did, at first, but now it's annoying. And the story behind it is kind of funny, but a lot to go into." I was about to say we should all talk about something else but Devon was still looking at me. I almost wanted to thank her and Katy because now that my injury was out in the open, I couldn't remember why it was so important to hide it. I felt better right away. Especially once I took off some extra layers. A well-regulated body temperature is way cooler than a "look." In this case, literally.

But Devon looked upset. She knew what my arm meant. Last year, she'd sprained her wrist scooping ice cream for a fund-raiser and had to sit out the regionals game.

"So, you won't be in the charity tournament?" Her mouth was turned down in a hint of a frown.

"What? What tournament?"

"We just found out about it from Coach Hollylighter in the hall," Mario said. He said that Piper Bell would be hosting a tournament that started next week. "It's going to raise money to help buy new playground equipment for a few older parks."

I would miss it. There was no way I could play with a

broken arm, even if it wasn't my pitching one.

But . . . . wouldn't a tournament be—to use Katy's mom's word—time-consuming?

"Well, now you have more time for your campaign," Johnny said, reading my thoughts. Or most of them. Because, like Katy, he'd planned on running, too. I had been putting off talking to him about whether he was going to do it because the whole thing was uncomfortable. I wasn't going to sacrifice a possible presidency for a boy, but I didn't want to create major drama, either.

"That's true," I said and, now wanting to get another weight off my chest, asked, "Are you still going to run, too?"

I braced myself for coming weirdness.

"Well, I love data and I'm really interested in seeing what students are thinking, statistically," he said. My stomach tripped over my lunch. Was I really going to face off against my **BOYFRIENDISH PERSON**? "But, really, that makes me a better campaign manager," he finished.

"You'll definitely run a great campaign," I croaked.

"But I'd rather be yours. Campaign manager, I mean," he said.

He didn't want to compete with me! He wanted to *help* me. He looked so cute and hopeful that I almost wanted to tell him to run for president so I could vote for him. I didn't, though, because Johnny **WOULD** be an awesome campaign manager. I had to scoop him up! "That would be great. If you really want to."

"Of course he does, he just asked you," Devon said, pushing some of the cafeteria's cauliflower mash around on her plate until it formed an orb the size of a baseball. "You've got my vote. But I wish you were going to be in the tournament."

I snapped out of the daydream I was about to have: a balloon drop during my victory speech wasn't over the top, right?

Mario heaved a sigh. "How are we gonna be in a whole tournament without Gabby?" he asked, and he looked really sad. See? Softie.

Devon cleared her throat meaningfully, and I knew the feeling. She was just as good as me, and Mario was acting like I was the team's only hope.

"I don't love it either, but we're going to have to figure it out," Devon said. "Are you sure your arm's broken?"

To answer that, I held up my bright orange cast. "You need sunglasses to look at that," Mario said.

"If it's an unofficial tournament, it's not such a big deal, is it?" I asked, knowing that if you played baseball the way Devon, Mario, and I played baseball, all your games were big deals.

"Not official, but who wants to bring a messy team to the field?" Devon said. "Will you at least come watch?"

Part of me hated the idea. *Watching?* Players didn't watch, they played! "I have the campaign to work on . . . ," I started. Johnny cleared his throat.

"I did some early math, and in the past, about sixty percent of the student body presidents also played a sport. It might be good to be seen at the field."

"How do you work so fast?" I asked Johnny. But maybe I could drum up some votes from the stands. I still had my right hand for handshakes. Handshaking was a crucial election thing. That had to be a sign.

A sign that I had to be destined for victory.

"I'll be there," I told Devon.

THE SCORE
Regular Eighth-Grade Gabby: 0
President Gabby: 1

THE GRAND-SLAM CANDIDATE

Goal: Knock the class president election out of the park
Action: Talk to my public and get my best minds on it!

Post-Day Analysis:
August 30

The packet I had to fill out was loaded with questions about my platform. At first, I thought platform meant something I'd need to stand on because I'm on the shorter side, but actually it means all **MY PLANS** for what I'll do when I'm president. I also have to "craft" a personal statement about my vision for the future: **THE WHOLE FUTURE**.

My platform can't be "I want to win because I like winning, even if there's more to life than winning."

Athletics *are* important to me, and I would like to make

it easier for everyone to do something sporty, but without the pressure of formal teams or the anxiousness of gym class—but sometimes people flinch when they hear the word *sports*. So, as I started to talk to the student body, I used my cast as a starting point.

When I told them I'd broken my arm at a baseball game and they said something like "oh no," I waved them off and said that sports were worth it. "I think Piper Bell should add some new sports to make it easier to play, even if sports aren't your thing. Frisbee golf! Competitive ball-room dancing! Archery!"

If someone said they didn't like sports, I'd say, "Do you know there are four hundred forty-two officially recognized sports but it's estimated there are one thousand five hundred sports around the world? There's probably one you like." Diego had told me that. His favorite was Hornussen, a game played in Switzerland with a puck called a "Nouss" that makes a whizzing sound.

"Like what?" a sixth grader who I approached on my way to geometry asked me. "I'm kind of a loner."

"Um, hmm, well . . . individual sports like bowling! Billiards! Ribbon dancing," I told her. "But if we had ping-pong or foosball tables in the atrium, you might be able to invite someone to compete. In a friendly way."

"Hmm," she said, smiling. "I'll think about it."

"Well, what issues are important to you?" I asked, feeling desperate for her not to walk away.

She thought about it for a minute and said, "I guess it would be nice if there was some kind of how-to thing for being a new student here. But not more orientations where it's all old people giving speeches. Maybe eighth graders, like you! My last school felt like home and now I feel lost."

"I was a new student here last year—well, a transfer," I said, and I told her my story. The short version, where I cut right to finding the talent squad before feeling like I belonged.

"See? Advice like that!" she said. "I already feel less lost."

"Maybe you're not a loner, either," I said. She told me her name was Rachel, and that she might show up for talent squad. Even without knowing who she'd vote for, I felt like I'd won somehow.

But the more people I talked to, the more I wanted to win. Not to win just for **ME**, either. It was like a magic spell; when I listened to someone, I could see their eyes get wide, like they couldn't believe I really wanted to hear what they had to say. And I did. My fellow students were awesome, and I wanted to make things better for all of them!

While I talked to students, Johnny polled people. Every time we saw each other, he had new percentages to rattle off—all informal, of course, even if they sounded very formal because of his tie. And because they were percentages.

"So sixty-three percent of student voters say that they normally don't pay attention to class elections because it's a popularity contest," he was telling me and Katy at my campaign headquarters, which was just an extra-soft couch in the school atrium that we used during study hall. "But the same sixty-three percent said a candidate who's available to hear their needs might change their minds."

Katy nodded. "That's so key. I want a good listener."

"Yes, that's high on the list of most desirable attributes," Johnny said, flipping to a new page in his clipboard. "And there's a strong showing for a candidate who will mix it up in the cafeteria—your Meatless Monday proposal is surprisingly popular—and while Sports for All sounded scary to thirty-two percent of a random sample, that **SAME** sample also overwhelmingly liked the idea of more casual athletic opportunities. Frisbee golf and ping-pong, especially."

"So . . . what does all that mean?" I asked.

"It means that, so far, you're a hit," Johnny said. He pointed at my arm. "People also liked your cast. It makes you seem down-to-earth."

"I was definitely down-to-earth when I fell on my face," I joked.

But seriously, I'm so excited about my reception by my fellow students I'm almost **GRATEFUL** for my broken arm. Ha! I'd managed to pull off the ultimate changeup and I wasn't even pitching! I'd turned my bum arm from a weakness into an *opportunity*.

It was better than turning lemons into lemonade. I turned a cast into a **CAMPAIGN**!

Regular Eighth-Grade Gabby: 0
President Gabby: 2 (and outstanding polling numbers!)

My Opponents

SMIRK

SMOOTH HAIR

Cassie Jacobs

Advantages: Smooth hair, knows all the good gossip

Slogan: Cassie. The only choice that matters.

Emerald Arcuno

Advantages: Artsy, interesting

Slogan: Emerald will make your days shine!

WILD CURLS

BIG GLASSES

NEAT HAIR

Cate Jones

Advantages: Excellent student, head of speech team

Slogan: Make this place great with a vote for Cate!

SUIT JACKET

There are no boys running this year, which isn't uncommon. I learned that Piper Bell used to be an all-girls school, and a boy has never won student body president! Interesting, right?

PITCH THAT PLATFORM

Goal: Toss the student body some plans so tempting they'll have to go for them
Action: Lock in my platform and make it official!

Post-Day Analysis:
September 1

I had so much good data from Johnny and great motivation from Katy that I was psyched. I spent a whole night carefully typing out my campaign materials (with one hand!) and narrowed down the key points of my platform: more casual athletic opportunities, some cafeteria menu updates (the veggie burger is a disaster, and fries need more dipping options), and more downtime for meditation and relaxation.

I also added an idea based on the talk with Rachel for

a student panel I was thinking of calling "New & You." Most of my plans were doable. The student government got to present to the Piper Bell Advisory Board, and I made notes on how to break each idea down into parts— the same way I played one inning at a time—so that doing them felt realistic.

For my explanation of why I was running, I said that I loved making plans and strategies—all **SUPER TRUE**—and my experience on the field would mean I could handle even tricky issues. "There's no such thing as a lose-lose situation, but I do believe in win-wins!" is how I ended it.

So, with a three-day weekend coming up, I was excited to tell my family about how I'd made the best out of a bad situation. Louie's favorite part of the Olympics is watching stories of competitors who've had to overcome really stressful circumstances, and now I had my own inspirational story. She'd probably cry a little.

For dinner, my dad had made homemade wild mushroom ravioli because it was easier for me to eat what I could spear with a fork.

"How was school today?" Dad asked me and Peter, who was decorating his pasta—he had plain elbow noodles in butter because he's so picky—with a blizzard of sprinkled cheese.

"We had a fire drill," Peter said. "But the best part was, something happened to the automatic locks on the doors and we couldn't get back inside for thirty minutes until the fire department came **AGAIN**, so we basically got double recess. **SO** awesome."

I sat patiently as Peter launched a five-minute Complaint Fest about how it had been hard to get a tetherball court. But my own news was so good that I was full of zen toward what passed as exciting in Peter's life. Double recess was nothing compared to my amazing campaign. When they rolled over to me, I even **SOUNDED** presidential when I said, "Well, the big news today is that I formally submitted my materials to run for class president." That's right, I used the words "formally submitted."

"Loser," Peter fake-coughed into his napkin.

"That's not what my polls indicate," I said. For once, I didn't have to roll my eyes at his insult. I had **DATA**.

"Wow," Dad said. "Polls. You sound like a real pro."

"I've been talking to so many people I didn't know," I said. "The election seems like a way bigger deal than I thought. But I think my chances are good. Johnny's been doing surveys for me and my ideas are a hit. And Katy is sort of my image consultant."

"That's incredible," Louie said. She wasn't misty-eyed like I'd hoped but she looked proud. "It's great to see you really throwing yourself into something new to you."

"She **IS** a pitcher," my dad said and laughed at his own joke. I gave him a chuckle, too, because my diplomacy skills were **ON FIRE**. Which is maybe strange because diplomacy means keeping your calm and dealing with situations in a sensitive manner. Fire is not exactly a calm thing.

I was so happy, it was like Seattle had never happened. But then . . . .

LIGHTNING CRASH!

Life is what happens when you're making other plans.

Or when your **PARENTS** are making other plans.

And they plan something that leads to your **WORST LIFE**.

"So I have some big news, too," my dad said, bringing out dessert: raspberry gelato from Gepetto's! As he placed bowls in front of me and Peter, I figured he was going to tell us about his next writing project, or some new recipe he was going to try, so I dug into my gelato. Like someone who doesn't know an **AWFUL TURN OF EVENTS IS GOING TO HAPPEN**.

"We are considering a move to Seattle."

The S-word! I almost spit out my gelato.

"That's hilarious!" I said, swallowing even though suddenly the gelato might as well have been mud. When my parents didn't say, "Got you!" I laughed again. This couldn't be real news.

But Dad and Louie were silent for a few seconds as they looked at me and Peter, who just kept eating his dessert.

Were they serious? They looked serious. But who would announce a move—or even that they are **CONSIDERING** a move—without getting their kids' opinions first? I was thirteen and even I knew that wasn't good parenting!

Then Louie reached for Dad's hand and said, "It would be a big change, but your dad's friend LaKesha . . ."

"Who I edited the book for," Dad chimed in. "She's the managing editor of the *Seattle Gazette*."

"She knows that your dad is also a heck of a writer . . . ," Louie said. She and dad were taking turns talking like they were recording a musical number, and it was making everything worse.

"And . . ." Dad was blushing. "I met her for lunch in Seattle."

"The day I took you kids to the aquarium," Louie added. I'd liked the aquarium. Well, not anymore, I didn't. The fish had been in on this whole awful plan.

"LaKesha said one of her sportswriters is retiring and she really wanted me to apply, so I did. I figured it was never going to happen . . ."

"But today she called and said he's a leading candidate."

I'M THE LEADING CANDIDATE, I wanted to say. Why had they even asked how our days were if they were just going to ruin them?

"So, in Seattle?" Peter asked, but not like he was upset, more like he was barely paying attention. Or maybe trying to conceal how happy he was that this news made me miserable.

"Yes, in Seattle," Dad said. "If everything works out."

If everything works out? Then **BOOM**? Seattle? It was like they'd already decided. How was that fair? It was like the other team deciding to load the bases before you'd even thrown your first pitch!

"I know it's out of the blue," Dad said, "but it's not the kind of chance you get every day."

"Your dad is really qualified," Louie added. "He's done a lot of sports features over the years, and this would be a chance to do more day-to-day coverage, too."

I shoved my spoon into the trick gelato and left it there. I didn't want any more. "But what about where we **LIVE**?" I blurted, upset when I heard the way I asked the question. I wanted it to sound different. When my parents thought I had a bad idea, they said things like, "Are you sure you've really thought this through?" I wanted to sound like that, but I couldn't make the right words get to my mouth.

Every second ticked in my head as I waited for my parents to say that I wasn't making sense, and of course we lived in Peach Tree. That they couldn't believe they'd used the word **MOVE**. Or that I was daydreaming again. (More like daynightmaring.) My skin got clammy all over, except under my cast, where my arm was hot and itchy. Everything was so confusing that Bob and Judy, the imaginary sportscasters who live in my brain, started to try to figure out what was going on.

Bob: *Gabby is really blindsided here.*

Judy: *Well, it's clear why. It's like she had home-field advantage and then the field got moved out from under her!*

Bob: *Like that trick where the magician pulls a tablecloth and everything on the table stays standing?*

Judy: *Bob, you really have a problem focusing, don't you?*

Bob: *That's a great trick. I love it.*

Judy: *Sorry, Bob, but I think Gabby is going to need to put her thinking cap on, not try to pull a rabbit out of it.*

My dad looked at me with the small smile that makes all his eye crinkles show. "I know, Gabs, this is a lot. And it's not definite, but it's a chance I never imagined having. No one wants to uproot you two, but we also would rather do this now instead of when you're in high school."

I felt a strange smile plaster itself on my face, and I couldn't uproot it.

Did I look **HAPPY** about this? I must have because my dad kept talking excitedly.

"I would be covering baseball—the Mariners—so when the team is on the road, we'd be able to come here for games and to visit, and Louie would keep her job but would work from home and be flexible enough that you two can do all the activities and sports you're used to. Just in Seattle, instead of here."

He and Louie went on and on and I felt like they were a light at the end of a tunnel but instead of going closer to the light like you're supposed to, I was flying backward out of the tunnel as their faces got smaller and smaller.

I know I said this playbook has helped me grow and get better at all this being-a-person stuff, but I'm not the Dalai Lama. I'm not even a regular llama, who, let's face it, seem like they'd be pretty good in a crisis situation.

DALAI LAMA

LLAMA

Dalai Lama Traits

Considered the human form of the Buddha of Compassion

Works to do no harm and only do things that help others

Excels at kindness to others

Owner of a mind at peace

Has a really nice smile

Llama Traits

Soft wool

Specially adapted feet, allowing them to navigate terrain from snow to sand (no hot dog falls!)

41

Complex stomach with several departments, allowing them to digest tough foods (bet they never get a bellyache!)

Very curious, very pleasant, will gladly approach humans

Excellent posture!

All I could do was stay still in my seat, listening to everything they said. Peter helped himself to more gelato, and instead of being annoyed with him, I was jealous of him. Why did he get to be so okay with whatever would happen? I hardly ever feel like that about anything! Like, Playbook, that's the whole reason you exist! Because I don't like surprises: I like plans, and strategies, not the whole game changing just when I think I figured out the rules!

And I definitely don't like my family playing an entirely different game—without me.

SCORE OF WHATEVER THAT WAS
Gabby: 0
Gabby for President: 0
Gabby's Life: 0

THINGS MY PARENTS SAID ABOUT CONSIDERING A LONG-DISTANCE MOVE

- "It's so exciting, and could be a huge adventure!"

- "If everything works out, it will be an adjustment, but we know you kids will eventually settle right in."

- "These things happen for a reason."

- "We don't mean for this to come as a surprise, but the opportunity came up so fast, we had to see what it could mean."

- "We might have to become Mariners fans!"

- "This could be **GREAT**!"

- "Do you want some more gelato?"

THINGS YOUR PARENTS SHOULD SAY WHEN THEY'RE CONSIDERING A LONG-DISTANCE MOVE

- "Just kidding! What kind of parents would do a thing like this?"

- "How will this affect *your* future?"

- "What do you think of Seattle?"

- "Oh, that's right: you hated Seattle. Let's just cancel this whole conversation."

- "We'd never make such a monumental decision without getting your thoughts first."

- "Will this ruin your life?"

- "How silly of us, of course it will ruin your life! You have everything going for you here!"

- "On second thought, we really shouldn't take you out of school and away from your friends."

- "We're incredibly sorry for even thinking about such a selfish idea! You definitely need more gelato."

EXPECT THE UNEXPECTED

"Expect the unexpected," some so-called ancient wise person once said.

You know what **THEY** didn't expect? That at this point, they're probably dead.

"You never know what awaits," everything in life tells you with a smile.

But the truth is that what awaits is garbage news on speed dial.

"Who knows what's around the bend?" you're told when you try to plan.

The secret is that what's around the bend is mostly poop hitting the fan (think about that!).

I thought I had things figured out, I thought that I could deal.

I even believed I could stay calm and wait for my arm to heal.

My life doesn't care, my plans don't matter, I'm not even sure
my world is round
Because just when I wanted to fly, I got knocked right down to
the ground.
"Expect the unexpected," is a thing you'll hear all the time.
You know what's unexpected? A poem that doesn't rhyme.

But gum on your shoe
Stepping in poo
Going on a trip and breaking your arm
Oversleeping your alarm
Missing the bus 'cause you're running late
Getting sick from something you ate
That feeling when no one can come to your party
Clouds in the sky when it's supposed to be starry
A terrible grade you can't improve
Your parents telling you that you might MOVE!

The unexpected isn't easy, like one and one is two.
The unexpected has a secret and I'll share it with you:
"Expect the unexpected" leaves you hoping for things to go
great.
But the unexpected is almost always news that you'll hate.

THE KNOW YOUR OPPONENT

Goal: Go up against Seattle in the battle for my life!

Action: Study up on my opponent to determine the best way to play it

Post-Day Analysis:

September 2

After my non-reaction at dinner last night, I just went to bed. I started texts to my friends but didn't know what to say. When Dad and Louie knocked on my door this morning, I'd pretended to be asleep, and I heard Louie say, "She must need to sleep in." What I needed was not to see them all weekend. I'd never been **SO ANGRY** at my parents before. That was the second-worst part of all this; the possibility of moving was still ranked at number one.

I had bad dreams. In them, I was in Peach Tree—my room was exactly the same, right down to the collage of Mo'Ne Davis tacked up above my desk—but out my window was nothing but the Space Needle, surrounded by the kind of gloom that looks like it can swallow you up. I called my friends (in the dream), but when they answered, they didn't even know who I was. I sent them texts with my picture, reminding them that I was still me, just far away, and all I got back were those three dots to show someone was typing . . . but no message.

So I finally texted Diego—in real life, not in the dream. He'd been worried about me since my arm incident. I think before it had happened, he'd believed I was invincible or something.

> Gabby: Bad news.

> Diego: Oh no, what happened? Is your arm okay? Is your other arm okay?

> Gabby: This is way worse.

> Diego: Oh no. Full-body cast? How are you texting?

> Gabby: We might be moving to Seattle.

Diego: That's an excellent birding city.

(I finally was getting used to the bird-watching hobby Diego had brought back from Costa Rica, and even supported his excitement over warblers and robins and feather texture and flight habits. But this was not the time . . . !)

Gabby: Diego! This is serious!

Diego: I know! I didn't know what to say! But u can't leave Peach Tree until college, or the majors. U r going to put this town on the map!

Ugh, he was right. I couldn't leave Peach Tree. I'd been thinking only of the immediate consequences and not how I was going to be a baseball star and Diego was going to rise to the top of the sportscasting game (unless he became a professional birder, which was **OKAY**). We had BFF goals that relied on me being **HERE**.

Gabby: There's no emoji sad enough for this.

Diego: You'll come up with something, right?

Gabby: I have to. But what?

Diego: I dunno. If u move, we'll still be BFFs.

Gabby: I know. But I don't want to move.

Diego: Hey, weird but Braves play Seattle today at 4.

Gabby: U just gave me an idea!

I switched from texting to the internet and did a search for Seattle and bookmarked pages that would be useful. Then I went to Instagram and found things hashtagged "Seattle," and also added Seattle on my weather app. Because this is how you did things in sports: before a big game, you learned all you could about your opponent. I've studied up on other batters and pitchers to see who on the team is a threat or might homer off me. In the battle of me versus Seattle, I needed to know my opponent.

There were a lot of grown-up news stories that might come in handy. Some director of something was mad about taxes, and some head of something else was saying the schools should be better, and everyone seemed to think home prices were too high and traffic was bad. But also, **YAWN**. I signed up for news alerts and hoped Godzilla would attack Seattle or something. I went downstairs to get some breakfast. If I was going to arm myself with facts, I needed brainpower.

"She's awake! We were worried you were going to miss the whole weekend," Dad said, looking too cheerful even for him on a Saturday. "How'd you sleep?"

"Fine," I said, sounding like I meant it. I put my phone on the counter to help myself to a blueberry muffin. "Good." *Fine and good for someone who's very angry at you!* I thought.

"And everything's okay?" Louie said. I could see from the look on her face that she was worried about me. Maybe after their big announcement last night she and Dad had realized how upsetting their news was. Still, if I told them now how much I didn't want to move, it would be like playing a game without warming up first.

"Sure," I said, taking a bite of muffin.

My phone dinged. Dad picked it up and handed it to me, but as he did, his eyes widened. "You're getting alerts from the *Seattle Gazette*?"

"Um, yeah, I, um, because you're going for a job there," I mumbled around bites of muffin. No way could I give away the real reason.

"Gabby, how wonderfully supportive," Louie said. She looked as happy as if I'd showed her a report card of straight As.

Dad put his arm around my shoulders and squeezed. "Thanks, kiddo. I was a little worried you'd be upset," he said.

"We thought you might be sulking in your room," Louie said. "But this is a very mature approach."

VERY MATURE? I wasn't being mature! I was gathering

evidence to show that they were dramatically altering the course of my life! All our lives! Or, possibly altering them!

"Who knows? By Labor Day weekend next year, we could be hosting a barbeque in Seattle," Dad said.

Who knows? I **KNOW**! I'm not doing anything in Seattle. **EVER.**

"If we move," I said, because I really wanted to keep that **IF** a big one.

"Yes, if we move," Louie said. "Whatever happens, we know you'll make good choices."

There it was, the exact reason why I couldn't throw myself on the kitchen floor and say I was never going anywhere. A tantrum was the opposite of a good choice, even if it was what I really wanted to do. Besides, tantrums are a rookie play.

My reconnaissance on Seattle wasn't going to be enough. Like in baseball, I couldn't just **KNOW** that a batter like

Mario was really good and I needed to throw my best stuff. I had to be ready in the moment. Sports are about more than facts; they are about **FEELINGS**. Every game, every play, was a little story, and you had to do the right things at the right moment to win.

I needed something bigger. I needed heart stuff, not just head stuff.

I went to my room and texted Katy and Johnny, separately. They needed to know what was happening.

Their responses were more proof I couldn't leave:

> Katy: Oh NO! We need you here! Plus, you're my fave collabor8er!!

> Johnny: Is it for sure? That's . . . not good at all. For everyone. But especially me.

I gulped as my inner Gabbys gathered themselves out of their sulk for a real moment of fizzy, roller-coaster romantic thoughts about Johnny that quickly ran off the tracks. I knew what he meant. We were just learning how to hold hands . . . How would we deal with long-distance romance? Still, romance . . . Were we like Romeo and Juliet, wrenched apart by our families? **THAT** had turned out awful. My flippy stomach-lifting feelings crashed down into total PITS thoughts of having to bail on my first boyfriend ever. And maybe my last. If everyone in

Seattle felt about me the way I felt about Seattle, I didn't have high hopes for my social life.

Because Johnny, as a math whiz, was reliably level-headed but also very good at solving things, I asked him what he thought I could do. But his response was more levelheaded than solution-y:

> Johnny: You can't really do much, can you? Maybe just make the best of the time you have left?

It was a very mature response. Mature. That word again. It was also kind of disappointing. But at least he followed it up with:

> Johnny: Maybe u can make it clear that it's much better if you can stay?

There was a prayer-hands emoji so I knew he really wanted it to happen. He was right. I had to find a way to stay. My friends all needed me. And I needed them.

I was on the stairs, ready to march down to the kitchen to tell my parents all the reasons this move would definitely ruin my formative years. (Not sure what *formative* means exactly but I know it's something parents say.) But then I heard my dad talking to Louie: "Is it just me, or are the kids taking this really well? Maybe we're doing the right thing."

Then Louie said, "I don't know. I'm sure it's not going to be **THAT** simple. But if we keep easing them into the idea, it might be smoother when you get the official offer."

"You mean IF I get the official offer. They still might go with someone local."

I kept forgetting that Seattle wasn't super official yet. Is it wrong to not want my dad to get the job? Because I don't.

Maybe a tantrum would help. If I stomped into the kitchen and put up a fuss, it would be clear, like Johnny said, that I don't even want to *consider* moving. But in a game, if an umpire makes a bad call—like says you're out when you think you're not—and you argue, you can make things weird with the ump. It's always worked better for me to just play harder and let the ump worry about his or her calls.

I needed my parents to see that Seattle was a bad call.

But how would I do that when they were so on the side of **TEAM SEATTLE**??

Seattle: 1
Gabby's Life: 0

PLAY ON, PEACH TREE!

CHARITY TOURNAMENT

8 GREAT TEAMS
FROM PEACH TREE AREA
MIDDLE SCHOOLS WILL PAIR OFF
TO PLAY BALL FOR A
GREAT CAUSE!

PLEDGE
FOR YOUR FAVORITE
TEAM IN ADVANCE!

◇ DONATE ◇
TO THE FUND-RAISER
ON EACH WIN
(FLAT DONATIONS ALSO
ACCEPTED & WELCOMED!)

• AFTER 2 LOSSES A TEAM
IS OUT OF TOURNAMENT PLAY

• TEAMS WITH THE BEST
RECORD AT THE END OF 3 WEEKS
(APPROX. 5 GAMES EACH) WILL
COMPETE FOR MEDALS

① ② ③

• BUT THERE ARE
NO LOSERS!

ALL FUNDS RAISED
GO TO PLAYGROUND
EQUIPMENT
AND FIELD TRIPS FOR
PEACH TREE AREA
KIDS' CLUBS!

HELP US
MAKE THIS
TOURNAMENT
A HIT!

THE CALL IT LIKE YOU SEE IT

Goal: Keep myself from getting too in the dumps about my (possible) move

Action: Make myself useful at the charity tournament, broken arm or not

Post-Day Analysis:
September 6

Since I wasn't going to throw a fit about Seattle, I did the mature thing: complained to everyone I knew that I would be leaving and moving to Seattle. Well, **MAYBE** leaving and moving to Seattle.

Complaining doesn't do a lot, actually. Still, it's nice to say every annoying thought you have about your annoying situation and have people listen and react, hopefully in a way that makes you feel like they really understand how cruddy things are.

It was not very presidential, however. Between third and fourth periods, I confused one sixth grader because I meant to talk to him about my candidacy and then I forgot and started telling him how awful my parents were. That might have cost me a vote. (Yes, Playbook, I'm staying in the election for now because I really want to believe **I'M NOT LEAVING**.)

But most of the reactions I got were the right ones: people were definitely devastated! I don't mean to sound excited about that, but it shows that no one wants me to leave.

NOOOOOOOO!!!!

DEVON

MARIO

DUMPSTER THE DOG

TALENT SQUAD LISA

COACH HOLLYLIGHTER

PIPER BELL LADY WHO PUTS FRUIT IN WATER

But none of them had **ANY SOLUTIONS**.

My broken arm wasn't helping things. Not that I could see anyone thinking, *Wow, your broken arm is really coming in handy during this challenging time!* But it was getting in the way. Getting a cast feels weird and awkward but getting used to a cast means you forget it's there sometimes.

WAYS A BROKEN ARM GETS IN THE WAY

- Petting animals

- Eating two-handed foods, like tacos

- Wedging yourself through narrow spaces

- Handling a pen or chalk

- Hugs!

I needed one of two things: the perfect plan to **STAY IN PEACH TREE**; or something to get my mind off the fact I might have to leave.

Devon handled my Seattle news with a series of blinks that seemed to say, "You can't let that happen." She asked what I was going to do, and because I still didn't have a great idea, I said, "Hope that my dad doesn't get the job, I guess?" Which also didn't feel great.

"Coming to the game today?" Devon asked, meaning the first tourney game. Since I have a broken arm, I'll be on the disabled list, even though Coach Hollylighter said I don't have to come if I don't want to. (But what am I going to do? I'm more than caught up on homework after avoiding my parents the rest of the weekend.)

"I was thinking I might work on my campaign speech," I said. All candidates had to give speeches next week and I wanted to give the best one.

"You really should be there." Devon will tell you exactly what she thinks if you ask her directly, but she doesn't always let on when she has something **SHE** wants. Her making two suggestions I come to the game meant she wanted me there for some reason.

"I can't even play," I told her. "And it's a charity game."

"Well, your fill-in is this seventh-grade transfer and I think he's starting today. Nolan Chao. I wanted you to see him. Maybe you'll have some pointers for him." Devon gave me her best pleading look, which just involved raising her eyebrows and basically daring me to say no.

A **FILL-IN**? Ugh. Thanks to my stupid cast, I was being replaced before I had even stepped totally out of the picture. I was in no mood to give pointers to some newbie. But now I was curious about Nolan Chao. "Fine, but I'm doing it for you, not my fill-in," I told Devon.

So, when four o'clock rolled around and my arm hadn't magically healed, I took a seat in the dugout, truly sidelined for the first time in my life. The stands weren't very crowded, maybe because a charity baseball tournament also had to compete with all the fall sports at Piper Bell, like soccer, lacrosse, and tennis.

I felt a little bad for the opponent, from Rockland: they had to be mostly sixth and seventh graders, and the Piper Bell team had a lot of eighth graders, so we looked a lot bigger and more intimidating. Had I ever been that small? (Fine, so I'm still kind of on the small side, but sixth-grade small is a **FEELING** more than a size. Even Diego, who's very tall, and Mario, who's very broad, can vouch for that.)

The Piper Bell players still hadn't emerged from the locker rooms, so I was the only one waiting on our team's side of the field, and each minute ticking by made me feel more abandoned than ever.

I was slumped against the back of the dugout like a forgotten equipment bag when Johnny showed up. I don't want to say like a knight in shining armor because— bleh—that's so old-fashioned and also because I knew why he was there. As our school's star mathlete, he also kept stats for a lot of the games. **BUT** this wasn't even an official game. I sat up straight. "I thought you'd be at the lacrosse game," I said.

"I thought . . . you might be here," he said, carefully writing "Piper Bell Charity Tournament Game One" across the top of his scoring sheet. "And might want company."

How did he **KNOW**?

"I do, since the team seems to have forgotten to show up, and also, I'm glad it's you," I said. Now I looked at my cast, where Johnny had written "Happy Healing." Every time we talked about feelings, or even things close to feelings, we both got shy.

Why was it so hard to say exactly what you meant to the person you liked? I kicked against the floor of the dugout with the tip of my shoe so the dust made a scratching noise. I was trying to think of what to say next when Piper Bell's team came onto the field.

"What are they wearing?" I said, even though I could see what they were wearing: **NEW JERSEYS**. Not New Jersey, the state, or its official clothing, but **NEW JERSEYS**. Jerseys I didn't have. Jerseys with an adorable image of our mascot, a penguin, on them.

THE JERSEY
A SIDELINED PLAYER
DOESN'T GET TO WEAR!

PIPER BELL

PENGUIN IN
A BASEBALL CAP
(IT'S ADORABLE)

"I think it's a new jersey for the tournament," Johnny said. "A new shirt, I mean, not a New Jersey like the Garden State."

"I can see that," I snapped, even though nothing was Johnny's fault. Then I quickly added, "I'm sorry. It's just way cuter than a cast. Ugh. I wish I could get rid of this thing and play ball!" I waved around the orange cast that somehow hadn't faded at all.

"The penguins are probably wishing someone knew they shouldn't be in Georgia," Johnny said. It was a home-run joke and got me to laugh until I saw the boy who had to be the new Piper Bell pitcher come out. My fill-in.

He didn't look nervous or worried at all. He was acting like he owned the place. Um, sound familiar? I had once been the pitcher acting like she owned the place. **ME.** Now, I knew better: Fields were for sharing. With your **TEAM**. Nolan sure didn't look like someone who was going to figure that out.

He went to the mound to warm up with Ryder Mills while the rest of the team filed into the dugout. "So that's him?" I whispered to Devon, who'd plopped down in the dugout with me.

"Yep, that's Nolan."

NOLAN CHAO

MY REPLACEMENT?

STATS:
HEIGHT... GABBY'S HEIGHT
BUILD.... GABBY'S BUILD
THE REST.. TOO EARLY TO
KNOW, BUT WHO
DOES THIS GUY
THINK HE IS ????

"Hmm."

He sure didn't look like someone who would want pointers from me. He looked like someone wearing the jersey I should have been wearing and feeling just fine about it.

He looked like someone whose parents could tell him he was maybe moving to Seattle and he would say, "Oh, okay, it will be no problem to leave all my friends and make new ones and start at another new school and find a new team and hop right over that dropped hot dog instead of tripping on it." Like a better **ME** than me.

Nolan checked out the field with satisfaction, like I had in my Golden Child days, or when I first started here (even though I was only pretending to feel that way). He didn't look like he was pretending.

As the first inning began, all the other sounds of the field and the crowd dropped away. I could only focus on Nolan and how easy he was making everything look in his brand-new Penguins jersey.

"Watch it," I muttered under my breath toward Nolan. "There could be a hot dog waiting to get you."

Johnny was scratching player names onto his stats sheet and looked up for a second. "Did you say something?"

I couldn't tell him how upset I was. It wasn't very sportswomanlike. So I shook my head. As Nolan easily struck out the first batter, Johnny said to himself, "If he keeps throwing like that, his ERA is going to be so low."

Old me, in case you've forgotten or the rules of baseball have changed a lot one hundred years from now (yes, I do plan on being a very old person), an ERA is an Earned Run Average, or how many batters get hits and score while you're pitching. If you're a pitcher, you want the number to be as low as possible, meaning you were effective at not giving away runs.

With the second batter up, Nolan wound up and threw. The batter, a girl with a long ponytail sticking out of her cap, **CRACKED** it far into the outfield, where Madeleine was not paying attention. Madeleine could be a weak link, but still, Nolan had really let that batter get a piece of it.

So much for his low ERA.

"It's a tournament **FOR CHARITY**, not to give away **RUNS**!" I muttered. Oh my gosh, I'd said it out loud. Johnny glanced at me and my insides curdled into something gross. He'd once told me I was a positive person and what if I'd just ruined it?

But he said, "You sound like me when the rest of the mathletes forget their pencils," and smiled, like he was glad we got upset at the same things.

Nolan didn't seem fazed by the runner, who'd made it to second. He composed himself and then struck out the next batter, then walked the batter after that.

"Whoa, his consistency is awful," I said to Johnny.

"It's his first game, so maybe he's nervous?" Johnny said.

"Nervous is one thing, but he looks sloppy," Devon said. I'd forgotten she was sitting next to me, because she'd gone into silent-Devon mode. "Ugh. Rookies. I'd help him but I don't think I can mentor **AND** bring my best game to the tournament. Can you?"

I nodded that I could, while wondering if teaching Nolan to be a solid replacement for me now meant I was helping him to replace me later?

As the team returned to the dugout for our at bat, I felt like Nolan was looking at me. SO I looked straight ahead, like he wasn't even there. It wasn't like he **KNEW** I was avoiding him on purpose.

We were at the top of the third and the only run was for Rockland.

"I hope we don't lose this game. Rockland's not even that good, and we went to regionals," Devon muttered, kicking the ground.

Johnny shook his head as Nolan made a wild pitch. "It's not looking good."

Coach Hollylighter, who grimaced as the ump called another ball for Nolan, peered over at me.

"Garcia, maybe you can talk to Chao?" she said. "I think he gets in his head a lot, like you."

I said, "Sure!" but I didn't mean it. When it had been **ME** coming onto the team as a new player, Coach Hollylighter told me to check my ego and build rapport with the team. Why wasn't Nolan getting the same treatment? But I didn't want him to fail, exactly, especially with Devon pouting beside me. After another runner scored in the third, I felt knotty in my stomach for the whole team, but especially Nolan. We were down 2–0 and if it hadn't been for another seventh-grade newbie making a double play at shortstop, Nolan would have let two more runs in. I knew how bad it could feel to pitch a lousy game.

I was trying to think of what to say, but in the fourth, Nolan let by only a single and no runs. "Hmph," Devon said. "Maybe he **WAS** just nervous."

Johnny nodded. "He's not looking bad."

Whose side were they on? And whose side was I on? I wanted a Penguin win, but I hated that my replacement would be responsible—even though two innings ago I'd felt bad for him.

In the fifth, Nolan knocked three batters out right in a row, and then Mario homered and drove in Madeleine and the new shortstop. We were up 3–2 and now Nolan looked relaxed in the dugout.

His fastball was speedy, and he even threw a couple curves that dropped just in time. The better he did, the less Nolan looked at me when the team came back to the dugout. And the more my teammates seemed to forget I was even there. Everyone backslapped and complimented each other and poured little cups of Gatorade—even Devon. I echoed every "way to go" and "nice hit!" but I wasn't wearing the uniform and it didn't feel like anything I did counted.

Being sidelined was like being the team's ghost. I was there in spirit but all the action passed right through me.

The Penguins won the game, 4–2, and Nolan beamed at each and every "nice going."

So Nolan Chao was just fine. And he sure didn't need pointers from me.

But I needed a plan to stay in Peach Tree because it was starting to feel like I'd never existed.

By next year at this time, everyone might have forgotten me, because the score was still:

Seattle: 1
Gabby's Life: 0

TEAM
GHOST GABBY

A FEW MIGRATORY* BIRDS OF THE UNITED STATES
(*OR, "DIEGO, THIS IS NOT MAKING ME FEEL BETTER!")

*MEANING BIRDS THAT LEAVE THEIR HOMETOWNS FOR VARIOUS REASONS BUT OFTEN COME BACK

- **Prothonotary Warbler**—A bright yellow little guy that feasts on insects and totally has to bail on Peach Tree for the winter so it can find bugs in Central America

- **The Buff-bellied Hummingbird**—Born in Texas but likes to head **NORTH** to hang out in the Northeast states. Maybe it's a Red Sox fan.

- **Bluethroat**—A rare bird in the US that hangs out in Alaska's tundra for a while but is so secretive, no one knows where it goes in the winter!

- **Phainopepla**—A bird with attitude! (See: shiny feathers and spiky head.) For part of the year, they feast on desert mistletoe in the Southwest and then move to oak and sycamore canyons. Scientists are baffled by the way they keep to themselves in one area and socialize in the other, and that they seem to "teleport." (Ugh, I need some teleportation powers!)

PHAINOPEPLA

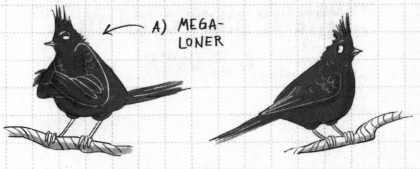

A) MEGA-LONER

B) SUPER-SOCIAL

IS THIS THE SAME BIRD?

THE IT AIN'T OVER TILL IT'S OVER

Goal: Find a plan for staying in Peach Tree
Action: Pay attention to everything

Post-Day Analysis:
September 9

"It ain't over till it's over" is a Yogi Berra saying, and one thing Diego and I agree on is that even though a lot of people claim Yogi never made sense, some things he said **DO** make sense, like this one. Even if, lately, my Peach Tree life is starting to feel like it's over. *Especially* today.

It started at breakfast. My dad has a habit of making big weekend meals, but what I saw downstairs a little while ago was way beyond the norm.

He was at the stove and next to him was an enormous stack of pancakes. In the middle of our table was a mixing bowl filled with cereal (no milk) and smaller bowls around it. It looked like a mix of Frosted Flakes, Froot Loops, and Cocoa Puffs.

Cereal Salad: It's Never a Good Idea

"Cereal salad," my dad said.

"But why?" I said. It didn't look that good to me. And any breakfast with the word "salad" in it was just plain unappetizing.

"We've got a lot of odds and ends in the pantry to use up so we won't have to pack them if we . . . ," he said.

"Seattle." It sounded like a swear word the way I said it, but Dad didn't notice.

"Yes, if it works out. Presumably. I spoke to LaKesha and she said we should hear something soon." **UGH**. "Presumably" still could mean "maybe" but it was a longer word and a grown-up one and I knew my dad wouldn't use it if Seattle wasn't becoming a more solid possibility.

Even without the cereal salad, my appetite was gone. Forget pancakes. Dad had made a Moving-Away Meal. I didn't want Pack-Your-Stuff Pancakes! Next it would be Say Farewell Falafel or Sayonara Spaghetti or Peace Out, Peach Tree Pork Chops. If I ate any of it, it would mean I'd accepted that we were probably going to move.

I took three pancakes and some syrup and put them on a plate that I brought to my room, where I'm writing this. (Fine, even when I lose my appetite I find it again pretty fast. It's like a boomerang. There's no way I'm starting a hunger strike to get my "No Seattle" point across.)

The past few days, I thought my parents would snap to their senses and say, "Oh, gosh, we can't leave Peach Tree!" Everything would go back to normal. My cast would come off and I'd maybe be class president and I'd play baseball and finish eighth grade at Piper Bell and . . . I don't know

SORRY FOR
SYRUP HERE.
(KLUTZY CAST
FINGERS!)

the rest **EXACTLY**, but the rest would be happening *here*, not Seattle.

Ping! My phone chimed with a text. Ack. A group text. Team sports I can handle, but group texts make me nervous.

> Diego: What are you doing today?

> Gabby: Pancakes now, later = ???

(I can't tell them about Cereal Salad.)

> Johnny: We were thinking about going to Peach Tree Preserve.

> Gabby: Who is?

> Katy: All of us.

See, the group text is instantly awkward! When did Diego, Johnny, and Katy talk about this? Was there another group text that I'd missed?

> Gabby: Is this a bird thing?

(If it is, I have to say, I am not in the mood.)

> Diego: Nah. No birds. Not formally. Unless you want to go birding, formally.

(This made me think of birds in formal attire. It's a little funny.)

Katy: She can't hold binoculars steady with a cast!

(This was technically not true. I could probably hold binoculars. But maybe Katy didn't feel like birding, either.)

Johnny: Are you in?

Gabby: Sure. In.

I know I probably should stay home today, until I figure out the play to help me stay home **IN PEACH TREE** for good. But with the way Dad is acting, I have no home-field advantage staying here. The Peach Tree Preserve is a pretty nature sanctuary with a small building for little kids with all kinds of displays about flora and fauna. Maybe it will inspire me with its wildlife and calming qualities.

(Pause for time with the flora and fauna)

I'm back, knowing what happens when you're "presumably" moving somewhere far away: your friends ambush you.

They **HAD** planned the preserve trip before asking me. Because it wasn't just a fun weekend hangout anymore. It was a **MEMORY LANE** hangout.

Johnny had packed a picnic for us. Well, okay, he'd ordered two pizzas from Peace-a-Pizza and brought some sodas, but if you're eating pizza in **NATURE**, it's a picnic.

So there my friends were, waiting for me on a blanket near the Tadpole Center, when I plopped down and said, "I didn't bring anything!" My dad would have probably let me clean out the pantry so we could just zip to Seattle on a moment's notice. I didn't say that.

"No, we wanted to do everything," Johnny said. He looked extra cute because he was wearing a ballcap over his floppy hair, which is not his usual look even though it could have been; ballcaps look great on him. ". . . 'Cause, you know."

That "you know" meant "because you're probably going to leave soon and we feel really sorry for you." Pity Party Alert! I reached for a slice of pizza.

HOW PIZZA WORKS:
(A QUICK GUIDE)

1. PIZZA IN NATURE:

PICNIC

2. PIZZA WITH FRIENDS AT A DINNER TABLE:

DINNER PARTY

3. PIZZA IN THE MORNING:

BREAKFAST

"Yum," I said, angling to bite down on a string of gooey cheese hanging from the end. Without a great Stay-in-Peach-Tree plan, all I had to work with was **TOTAL DENIAL** that anything was happening.

Until . . .

ME AT MY BEST ANGLE (NOT)

JOHNNY LOOKING CUTE

"Wait!" Katy said, snapping a picture of me sitting next to Johnny on her phone. I basically had my mouth open eight thousand degrees while Johnny smiled.

"This might be your last Peace-a-Pizza," Diego said. "We're going to commemorate everything. I mean, I know we'll still be friends, but we thought you might like it. Memories."

Here's what was going through my head as he said that:

Bob: *Do you feel that, Judy?*

Judy: *I do. Gabby is PEEVED.*

Bob: *Let's look at why this play on her friends' part is not going to score them any points.*

Judy: *It should be obvious to them. Gabby doesn't want to go . . .*

Bob: *But here they are, planning special events and a photo project!*

Judy: *Commemorating, Bob! They're acting like she's almost gone.*

Bob: *We know it comes from a better place than that.*

Judy: *Yes. But they should know Gabby better!*

Bob: *It's like they think she's not going to* **FIX THIS**!

I wanted to scream, "Why are you trying to get rid of me! I'm not going anywhere!!" Instead, I very calmly nibbled another corner of my pizza and then said into my friends' kind, pizza-chewing faces: "Guys, just because it **SEEMS** like I'm moving, we don't even know that it's final. My dad applied for the job but there's still a chance he won't take it. Why would he? They don't have pizza like this in Seattle . . ."

And, as I said that . . .

A lightbulb went off in my head. No, wait, everyone is saying that wrong: a lightbulb went **ON** in my head. A whole scoreboard's worth of lightbulbs. They went on and then they got so bright, I was pretty sure my friends could see all the weird crevices of my brain right through my skull. That sounds disgusting but the inner workings of amazing things can't all be beautiful.

"**THAT'S IT!**" I said.

"Did you burn your tongue?" Katy asked.

I shook my head and said, more and more excited as my idea took shape, "I'm not going anywhere."

"Huh?" Diego said.

"But your parents . . . ," Katy said.

"Isn't it your dad's dream job?" Johnny asked.

"Those are all factors," I said, and I felt so inspired that I got to my feet. Some little kids at the nature center actually turned away from the lily pad pond to stare at me. "Seattle has some pros. Or one pro. The job."

"But," I went on, feeling so brilliant I might have been outshining the sun, ". . . the point of a pros-and-cons list is to see which option has the most pros."

"Sure," Diego said. "But like Johnny said, it's your dad's dream job."

"But it's in Seattle. Which has no other pros, and mostly **CONS**. What if I make my parents see there are only **PROS** to living in Peach Tree?"

I'd been studying up on Seattle, but I had been looking at this all wrong. I didn't have to make it a choice between me and Seattle. This was a competition between Seattle and Peach Tree. And that wasn't even a contest.

"If you can really fill up an all-pros column, then the math is good," Johnny said, nodding to Katy and Diego. I could have kissed him. But not really, because we haven't exactly kissed yet. Which is another reason I want to stay in Peach Tree. I can't just jump states when I may be on the verge of my very first kiss, right?

"Of course the math is good, because Peach Tree is where we belong," I said. I took another bite of pizza to celebrate.

"But don't you think maybe your parents already did a pros-and-cons list? Or talked about it?" Katy said. I could see from the look on her face she thought I was getting carried away.

"You're right," I said. "It can't just be a list. I need **EVIDENCE** to prove it." I didn't say, "I need a play or two to prove it," because you're still super top secret, Playbook.

I took a picture of my friends looking at me with definite awe in their faces. Now I had something worth commemorating: the moment when **I FIGURED EVERYTHING OUT**.

And that, Playbook, is how I begin my next official Season of Gabby. The play will be called . . .

The All-Pros Play!!!!!

THE ALL-PROS PLAY!

Goal: Make my parents see there are only pros to staying in Peach Tree, meaning it beats Seattle any day

Action: In a multiphase **SUPER PLAY**, devise several scenarios to demonstrate Peach Tree's pros, in a way my parents won't even know it's happening

Post-Day Play Development Analysis:
September 9 (cont'd)

This is it. I can feel it. I won't be moving to Seattle. Finally, I have the right mind-set: This isn't about me versus Seattle or me versus my parents. It's about Seattle versus Peach Tree. If anyone can make Peach Tree a winner, I can.

    Bob: *Judy, I think we witnessed some Gabby history in the making when she stumbled on this play.*

Judy: Let's take a look at that clip again.

Bob: Gabby is doing some of her best work AND thinking with an injury.

Judy: It is impressive, but I'm still curious: How can she do this?

Judy doesn't know me. Well, she does. She's in my head and I more or less invented her, but Bob and Judy talk the most when I'm doubtful. And I shouldn't be doubtful, right?

Since the move was related more to my dad because he was the one going for the job, I started to make a list of everything my dad likes about Peach Tree. It wasn't that Louie's input didn't count, but if she was willing to change around her life and her fancy job—which she loved—to support Dad in his new one in Seattle, then she was already mostly convinced. So the focus was on him. He needed to see that taking the job would mean leaving too much behind. If Dad started to worry about leaving Peach Tree, it was easy to imagine Louie saying, "We don't have go, you know." So here's my short list of Peach Tree things Dad likes:

- The library, where he does some of his writing and volunteers as an English tutor.

- Walker Park—the biggest park in Peach Tree, where he jogs (weird, right, since it's called Walker?) because the dirt trails are perfect on his knees. (Also, it has benches in the shade, and since he really doesn't **LIKE** jogging, he loves those.)

- Grandma Garcia—Also known as Abuelita Salma, Dad's mom, who technically lives in Florida but gets to visit us a lot. Seattle is not close enough to drive in for a weekend.

- Gus's Butcher Shop, Sunshine Produce, Fay's Market, the Peach Tree Farmers Market—I know Seattle has plenty of food, but for Dad, going shopping for ingredients is about the **PEOPLE**. He loves that everyone at these places knows him, and if you go with him when he shops it takes **FOREVER**.

I know I need more, but this is a start. Let me think . . . (Pause for think break)

EEK! IT'S SEPTEMBER 10!

That think break went into extra innings—and there's still no winner!

Playbook, my thinking isn't going well.

I THOUGHT ALL NIGHT. (Or, the parts of the night before I fell asleep with no ideas.)

But instead of ideas, all I could think of was everything I would lose if this play doesn't work.

My room: I can take all of the stuff in it with me, but there's no guarantee that my Mo'Ne Davis poster will still be in a spot the sun hits each morning. And I won't wake up with a view of my favorite tree, or the same curly shadows.

My friends: I know I won't **LOSE** them, but we'll probably lose track of each other, at least a little. It was hard enough when Diego was in Costa Rica for a few months. I'd be gone **FOR GOOD**.

My school: I was finally feeling settled in at Piper Bell. Better than settled. I might be **PRESIDENT**. Piper Bell matters to me or I wouldn't be running for president.

My team: The Penguins—more than any team I've been on—feel like **MY TEAM**. We have rapport, or have it when I'm not benched. I thought rapport was silly when Coach Hollylighter first brought it up but I get it now.

Remember how, when I first got transferred to Piper Bell, it was when I was on a life win streak? Well, moving to Seattle would be worse. It wouldn't break up a win streak. It would break up **MY LIFE**.

So here I am in Life Studies class, sneakily writing this while we watch a video on how to make a budget. (But, technically, the list I just made **IS** studying my life.)

Life Studies is a class that's always changing because, as Piper Bell once said, "as the world grows, so do we." She wanted students to be well-rounded in every way, so Life Studies teaches all this boring grown-up stuff like how to be careful with money, how to have good basic manners (not frou-frou stuff with weird forks but like how to write a thank-you note when someone helps you with something), or how to create good habits or eat a balanced diet for energy blah blah blah. Everyone has to take it. Later in the year, we get to learn the Piper Bell Basics, a bunch of things every human should know how to cook. You make eggs three ways and an easy sheet cake and a protein bowl (vegetarian if you want) and other stuff.

I had this whole vision of how it would be like being on a cooking show with my friends, and it's another thing I might miss.

"Psst." Katy sits behind me and she's poking me. "This might be your last Life Studies class."

"I'm not moving tomorrow." Or ever, I wanted to add. But being idealess for the All-Pros Play was making me nervous.

Johnny peered back at us and sneaked his phone out of his backpack. My phone vibrated in my bag with a message from him. Katy's too. We both sneaked our phones out.

> **Maybe your last Life Studies video about budgeting?**

I was about to make this the first Life Studies class where I ran screaming from the room.

It was almost like they **WANTED** me to move.

"Do I see phones out?" Our teacher, Mr. Bogado, was suddenly standing over my desk, looking from me to Johnny to Katy. "This is a warning. If I see them again, there will be an After-School Think-About-What-You-Did Session."

(Piper Bell is a progressive school, but that doesn't mean progress like you can use a cellphone in class; it just means they don't call detention Detention.)

MR. BOGADO

LIFE STUDIES TEACHER

Height: Currently looming

Build: Muscly (he used to play college football)

Excels at: Fancy footwork. As a running back, he also took ballet classes.

Favorite Athlete: Esther Williams, swimmer and swim-dancer in old movies. (He has a big picture of her at the front of the class.)

Motto: "The wisdom acquired with the passage of time is a useless gift unless you share it." —An Esther Williams quote he has above the whiteboard

"It could be your last After-School Think-About-What-You-Did Session," Katy said.

"It would be my first," I hissed to her. "And yours. And Johnny's. I don't think it's something to aim for."

Mr. Bogado nodded at me. He gave us one long look before returning to his desk.

It did occur to me that I could start getting in a lot of trouble and then my parents would have to put all their energy into reforming me. Or it could make them think I need a "fresh start," with Seattle as the perfect spot for it. I wouldn't make a good delinquent anyway.

(Playbook brainstorm pause as I try to avoid a Think-About-What-You-Did Session)

So, after a day of no ideas, I'm back in my room. A full twenty-four hours **WASTED** without any plans created. Playing baseball would help me think. That sounds weird, but when my brain is all musty and slow, playing ball is the way I clear out the cobwebs. But I can't. I can't throw. I can't go to the batting cages. I can't even put my mitt on because my left hand is trapped in a cast.

Pacing! People pace when they're thinking.

(Pause to try pacing)

Whoa.

There I was, pacing my room like you see people do when they're trying to **SOLVE A HUGE PROBLEM**.

And, maybe I was muttering to myself.

I was definitely muttering to myself. Maybe doing whatever's louder than muttering. I was trying to think about the All-Pros Play like a baseball game.

"What will make Peach Tree a sure winner? What's my home-run move? Where is the **SWEET SPOT**?"

There is a store called the Sweet Spot, and it does have the weird old candy Dad likes. (Not old as in sitting there but old as in what he ate when he was a child four million years ago. Person-ally, I think candy has come a long way, but maybe if you grew up liking weird spirals of black licorice, you can't develop a better sense of taste later on.)

Seattle probably has old candy, too. But, by sweet spot,

SOMEWHERE AROUND HERE IS THE SWEET SPOT

WHEN YOU FIND IT = A BIG HIT

I mean the baseball kind. The sweet spot is about your bat, and how to use it optimally.

People have all kinds of takes on it, and there are even formulas and angles and equations to determine a bat's sweet spot. Once you think you have the answer, you could still find a second sweet spot on the same bat!

It can be the place where, when you hit the ball, the bat vibrates the least and your hands won't sting when you **THWACK** a ball really hard.

It can be the section of the bat where the maximum amount of force is transferred to the ball, and you make it go farther.

It's all very scientific, in a way, but like a lot of science things, it's a little bit magic, too. (Rainbows, for example, have a totally scientific explanation but are also magical when you see them.) The way I think of sweet spots (and I pitch more than I bat, so in some ways, I would rather bats' sweet spots remain mysterious and unknowable!) is: they are the points on the bat that will give a batter the maximum performance and/or the minimal sting.

So, I need to find all the Peach Tree sweet spots: things that would go a long way toward convincing my dad and Louie to **STAY PUT** but that would leave them feeling **NO REGRET** for bailing on this Seattle talk. Maximum good vibrations, minimum sting! If I could find them, my dad would realize there's no better bat—I mean town—for him. And us. Because, as he and Louie seemed to be forgetting, we are a family!!

"Sweet spots. Peach Tree sweet spots," I was saying as I paced. I was getting really good at pacing.

Then, Peter walked in.

PETER! WALKED! IN!

He just barged in like he lived here. Okay, this is his house, too, but it's **MY ROOM**. There's a sign on the door that specifically says: **YOU ARE CROSSING THE LINE INTO GABBY'S STRIKE ZONE. IF YOU ARE FOUL (PETER!!), YOU MUST KEEP YOUR MITTS OUT OF HERE.**

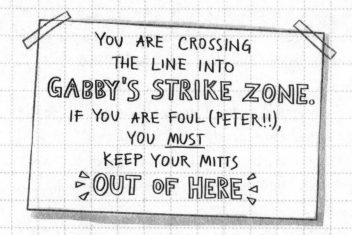

YOU ARE CROSSING
THE LINE INTO
GABBY'S STRIKE ZONE.
IF YOU ARE FOUL (PETER!!),
YOU MUST
KEEP YOUR MITTS
OUT OF HERE

(From a baseball standpoint, the sign doesn't make a ton of sense, I know.)

"Go away," I said. It's a reflex for whenever I see Peter coming. Or hear him breathing.

Peter raised his chin at me and said, "No." He was dribbling a soccer ball between his feet, something he does often that seems to relax him. (It's also something that is totally unfair because I'm not allowed to throw a ball in the house, which would relax **ME**.) "I can hear you talking to yourself, you know."

Oh, great. The last thing the All-Pros Play needed was Peter ratting me out to Dad and Louie. The plan working relied on them thinking I was okay with the move—Dad especially. My sweet spots had to surprise him and make him think **HE** was bonkers to want to leave Peach Tree. I needed to give him the kind of reminders that didn't stick like a Post-it Note but lightly tapped him on the shoulder without letting him know I had **ANYTHING** to do with them.

"Stop spying on me," I said, and I closed you, Playbook, and kicked you under the bed (sorry for that).

Peter rolled his eyes. "I'd rather ignore the sound of your voice. But I heard you. You're trying to stop us from moving."

I shook my finger at him angrily. "You don't know what you're talking about," I said. I almost added, "One day, you'll understand."

Because of course Peter didn't understand **NOW**. Peter was fine with moving. He thought Seattle was so great and perfect and he had his dumb Space Needle snow globe front and center on his dresser like he couldn't wait to stand under the real thing again.

"You're looking for a magic thing that will make Dad and Mom want to stay here."

"Pffftttttt," I told him, trying not to deflate like a balloon. "Why would I even think I could do that?"

Peter looked down and kicked the soccer ball from foot to foot.

Taptaptaptaptaptaptap tappity-tap tappity-tap.

The rhythm was soothing, and I was jealous. If my mitt could fit over this bulky cast, I'd be able to squeeze it open and closed and feel like I was thinking straight. Instead, I was thinking in zigzags and spirals and loops.

Bob: *Gabby is being caught out, right now . . .*

Judy: *What will she do if Peter foils her play before she even starts it?*

Bob: *Judy, I don't want to think about it. How will we make it in Seattle?*

Judy: *Our skills translate, Bob. But we both know you're sentimental.*

Bob: *So are you.*

BOB   JUDY

⋛INSIDE GABBY'S BRAIN⋜

Peter couldn't screw up the All-Pros before I even gave it a shot! I was incredibly sad but also **AGITATED** (one of this week's English Comp vocabulary words), and while Bob and Judy bawled, the little Gabbys angrily stomped around like they'd like to go head-to-head with Peter.

It was too many feelings at once, and I was desperate to make Peter go away. "I can't stop us from going to Seattle," I said.

Peter stopped the ball beneath his foot, and when he finally looked up, he didn't have the expression of someone who was going to run off and tell on his sister. (I'd seen that look before.) He looked **CONTRITE** (another new vocab word, which can mean guilty or apologetic, but also sheepish—Peter might have been all three).

"I just figured if anyone knew how to keep us from going, it was you," he said, really softly, like he didn't want to admit this. "I know you make . . . **PLANS**."

"They're plays," I snapped, but then I felt bad because he looked so uncomfortable to be in my room, saying nice things. And then I got nervous because he doesn't know about you, Playbook, or the plays you contain. "And why would you come to **ME** about not going to Seattle? Are you trying to make me talk, so you can rat me out?"

Peter was quiet for a few seconds and I thought he **WAS** going to tattle, but then he said: "The truth is, I don't want to go to Seattle, either. I like it here. I don't want to leave."

Playbook, I believed him. I know that goes against everything I've ever said about my lying, annoying, irritating, pestering, ill-willed, sometimes-smelly little brother (who is **AS TALL AS ME**, which is a betrayal on its own), but I did.

I believed him.

"Okay," I said, finally. The thing I said next felt like someone else was saying it, even though I could feel words come out of my mouth: "I'll tell you what I'm doing."

I poked my head into the hall for signs of Dad and Louie and then shut the door. For some reason, I was welcoming Peter into my room, because when the world has gone topsy-turvy on you, you do weird stuff. "But before I do, we're a . . . team now."

I held out my right hand—my pitching hand, my not-in-a-cast hand—for him to shake. And we did.

I shook hands with my little brother.

AM I <u>SURE</u> ABOUT THIS???

AN UNLIKELY, UNNATURAL ALLIANCE

"So . . . team?" I said. A team. With Peter. What was happening? I felt like I might vomit up the hot dog that I'd tripped over.

"Team . . . ," Peter said, and it made me feel better that he looked as sick about it as I felt. "So what's the play?"

"I call it . . . the All-Pros Play."

Playbook, he liked the idea. I didn't tell him about you, exactly, but I told him that I use plays to come up with actions and goals and strategies to make my life a win. Or, okay, when it can't be a win, at least a good effort.

We agreed to think about sweet spots and go over them in a few days. I never thought I'd say this, much less write it, but I think Peter is going to be a good teammate.

Or at least highly coachable.

THE REAL COMPETITION BEGINS!
Peach Tree: 1
Seattle: 1
(Maybe?)

AN UNLIKELY ALLIANCE

For nine years now . . .
My brother has been my bother,
And no it doesn't matter
He was made by my stepmother
And my father.

He's pulled my hair
He's broken my toys, he's mocked
And rolled his eyes
He's made me feel like a joke
And he keeps fresh insults stocked.

He gets to do whatever he wants
My parents say he's the baby and so sweet
But they're clearly overlooking

All his worst tricks and stunts
(Plus the size and smell of his feet).

He's been a pain in the morning
In the night and the afternoon
He's been a pain through every hour
And that takes real might
Even for a goon.

Now he wants to work with me
And admit this, I will.
If he puts half the work into this plan
As he did for making up names for my last zit
We could put this move at a **STANDSTILL**.

So can my fiercest enemy
Really swear to now be my trusted ally?
Is he plotting to mess up my plan
And only pretending to care . . .
Or is he a good guy?

THREE STRIKES AND WE COULD HAVE BEEN OUT

Goal: To **NOT** reveal to our parents that Peter and I are up to something
Action: Stop being nice to each other

Post-Day Analysis:
September 11

Buddying up with Peter had one major hazard: I was buddying up with **PETER**.

Three times today, things almost got ugly. Three strikes, but fortunately, our parents didn't quite catch them.

Strike One! Breakfast:

Dad was making bacon, and when Peter went to put some on his plate, he offered me first bacon. "Gabby, do you want any?"

Dad's and Louie's shocked expressions would have been priceless if they weren't a red alert that they might catch on to us.

Peter's nice gesture was like a line drive straight for me: I had to act fast! So, I caught it and lobbed back, "What'd you do to it?" I made emergency eyes at him.

"Like I was actually going to give you **FIRST BACON**! You fell for it. **HA!**" Peter said, thinking quick.

Strike Two! After school:

Peter was working on a book report for Ms. Kline, who'd been one of my favorite teachers. He was at the kitchen counter, with the book next to him. I picked it up.

MS. KLINE

ENGLISH TEACHER

Height: 5'5" but seems taller due to Teacher Bump

Build: Wiry (Ms. Kline runs marathons)

Favorite Sport: Running but also attends a weekly roller-skate dance.

Favorite Athlete: Serena Williams

Motto: "First

forget inspiration. Habit is more dependable." —Octavia E. Butler

"You got to read *Where the Mountain Meets the Moon*, too? I loved that book." I picked up his copy from the counter.

"It was so good," Peter agreed. "It would be so cool to know the Man in the Moon. We'd have all the answers."

"I've always felt that way. And isn't Minli's dad the nicest?"

"Totally!" Peter agreed.

There we were, hanging out at the dining room table, on the verge of a mini book club, when Louie walked in with her friend Patrice, who always makes comments about how Peter and I don't get along.

Prim & Pristine
Patrice

THE REAL ESTATE AGENT

NEVER A HAIR OUT OF PLACE

VERY NOSY →

SAYS SPORTS ARE "TOO MESSY"

ALSO, LOUIE'S FRIEND

She's also a real estate agent so seeing her walking around our house now gave me the chills.

"Would you look at that, Louie? Are your kids getting **ALONG**?" She said it like we weren't even there. I'm really not sure why Louie likes Patrice.

"It's **MY** book," Peter said, swiping the paperback from my hand, thinking quick.

"I guess I spoke too soon," Patrice said to Louie, who made a **"CUT IT OUT"** gesture at me and Peter. "But those countertops! A potential buyer will love those," she said, then eyeballed the supplies from my president poster-making still in one corner. "Once that clutter's gone, of course."

See? She's the worst.

Strike Three! Bedtime:

Normally, if I use the hall bathroom for any amount of time (to deal with my hair, which doesn't follow the laws of nature or even detangler spray), Peter stomps past at least three or four times, just to be annoying. But today, as I was working a new cream into my curls (before bed, so my hair has the whole sleep cycle to maybe follow directions), the hallway was silent.

Then I heard Dad on the landing. "Peter, you okay?" In our house, Peter **NOT** making a ton of noise is more alarming than if he were.

I couldn't hear if Peter answered, so when the coast

was clear, I knocked lightly on Peter's door. He opened it a crack. "I almost got caught making my list!" he said.

"We need to stick to our normal habits," I warned him. "They'll catch on if they think we're buddies."

A hurt look flashed across Peter's face. "I mean, if they think we're a team," I said, to be clearer.

"But we kind of are buddies, too, right?" Peter was standing there in his old soccer ball pajamas and he looked little to me, even though he was my height and the pajama pants were too short on him. He wanted to be buddies?! Everything was **SO. WEIRD.**

"Yeah, of course we are," I said, wondering if I meant it and thinking that I did.

Now Peter smiled. "I'll try to do a better job. I'm just so excited about the plan that I'm not acting like myself."

"Have you thought of anything?" I asked him. I still had **ZERO** ideas, but I didn't want to tell him that.

"Not really," he said. "Have you?"

I peered around for signs of our parents. "Not exactly, but I will. **WE** will," I said and gave Peter a reassuring pat on the arm. A coach's second job is to make her team feel like winners. Her first job is to make her team glad they're on it. "We'll meet in a few days. Just keep everything under you hat till then."

SUPER FROM THE SIDELINES

Goal: Find the home-run idea for the All-Pros Play
Action: Open my mind to a great idea by letting my thoughts wander as a benchwarmer

Post-Day Analysis:
September 13

If it weren't for having Peter on my side the last few days, things would be grim. Dad is still in pantry-cleaning mode and I've caught Louie looking at houses in the Seattle area on her phone more than once. (All the houses are **TERRIBLE**, if you ask me. Even the ones with giant backyards. Because the backyards are in **SEATTLE**.) **THEY SAY** nothing is for sure, but **THEY ACT** like the move is happening.

The problem is, I told Peter we'd figure something out but I'm **STILL** stumped. The pressure is on to have good ideas for the All-Pros Play by tomorrow, and since sitting in my room hasn't drummed up any big brain moments, I decided to go to the baseball game, the third one of the tournament. At the second game, with Devon pitching, I'd been a better bench rider. Devon had gotten a win against a team from Hillside, and because she wasn't my **REPLACEMENT**, Nolan, I could be happy for her. Piper Bell was up in the tournament with two wins.

Now, we—or Piper Bell—would play **LUTHER**. The Luther Lions. My old school's team. I would have loved to be pitching. Instead, I'd probably have to watch **NOLAN** pitch to my old team.

I'll admit it now, but for a quick second, I thought about bailing on the game. Until I saw some writing across the top of a blackboard inside a classroom near my locker: "It's a good thing to clear the mind sometimes. It makes room for new ideas." It was something Piper Bell, the lady our school is named for, once said.

If I didn't think too hard about Nolan, maybe the game would clear my head and a good plan would beam into my brain.

I decided not to sit in the dugout this time, so I wouldn't feel like a ghost again. But from the stands, it was hard to clear my head, or get a clear view. The bleachers were **PACKED**. With the tourney in full swing (ha!), there were even vendor booths and a concession stand. My baseball brain kicked into gear, and my mitt hand tingled. The only thing on my mind was wishing my arm was in the right shape to play.

Diego was there, covering the game for the *Luther Bulletin* (it was a step down after his summer job as a *Peach Tree Gazette* junior reporter, but Diego wasn't in it for the title). He waved me over to the stands, and as I walked over, I could hear him talking to an old man about birding. Diego's newish hobby was like everything with Diego: he had to tell the world about it.

The man asked if other kids liked bird-watching as much as Diego did. And Diego said, "I hear some jokes, but I don't let it ruffle my feathers."

To go along with him, I added, "Do you call people who tease you mockingbirds?" But Diego and the man looked at me like I was wearing ski gear on a sunny day. But **MOCKING**-bird, get it? Ha. (For not being a birder, I'm really great at bird jokes.)

GABBY GARCIA'S ORIGINAL BIRD JOKES

- What do you call a bird that doesn't own its nest? A wren-ter!

- What do chickens use to dye their feathers? Henna!

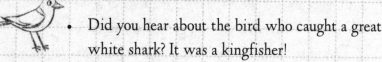

- How did the inexperienced sparrow win her first baseball game? By winging it!

- Did you hear about the bird who caught a great white shark? It was a kingfisher!

- What did the nocturnal bird say about its invitation to a sleepover? Owl be there!

I waited for Diego to get the joke. Sometimes he misses them. When he finally laughed (took him long enough!), his face turned serious. "Your mom told my mom about the maybe-Seattle thing," he said. "We'll need to really ramp up our last Gabby moments."

"Did you forget about the plan? The All-Pros Play? Pet—" I stopped. Diego would never believe I had things under control if I told him I was taking Peter's help.

"I didn't forget and I hope it works, but Mom even said it would be a great adventure for you. It is a little exciting, don't you think?" How could Diego say that?

"Sure," I lied. How was it possible the only person I was seeing eye to eye with lately was **PETER**?

Diego pointed at the field. "Luther looks good today.

I'm lucky you're not pitching; I wouldn't know what team to root for."

"Don't worry," I said. "You'll get a chance to make that decision when you watch me pitch against Luther this spring." Diego might not have faith in the All-Pros Play, but I still could remind him I wasn't backing down.

"For sure," Diego said. His voice still had that unconvinced tone. But he would see soon enough that I knew what I was doing.

I headed up the bleachers where Johnny was showing the clipboard ropes to a younger mathlete. Next to her was Katy, who'd brought some of the new talent squad members. I'd had to pass on the meeting today, and I wasn't expecting to see her.

"Hey, guys, what's up?" I was turning my frown upside down. Diego and my friends could plan all the memory lane events they wanted, and I'd use them as motivation to make my plan work. My plan and Peter's. If Peter and I could find ways to get along, why shouldn't we be able to convince our parents to stay in Peach Tree?

Johnny looked up from his clipboard: "Have you been talking to people about the new cafeteria options idea? Because there was a poll on the Piper Bell student social page and that idea ranked the highest. You're leading."

I'd already seen the poll, but I pretended to be surprised. "That's great news!" I said.

Then I saw The Look. Same as Diego's. I knew Johnny was thinking of asking me if I'd still be running if the move became definite. Little did he know, **THIS** candidate wasn't taking those questions today. Instead, I turned to Katy and the new talent squad kids. "Hi, I'm Gabby Garcia," I said, with my best Vote for Me smile. I had Confidence Squared, and that's math it doesn't take a Johnny-level brain to understand. I'd make everything work. Even the campaign, which needed my attention. I beamed even harder. "I'm on the talent squad, too."

"This is who I was telling you about," Katy said. "Gabby is a pitcher, too. These newbies need some fresh

KATY & TALENT SQUAD

inspiration. So do I. All my songs lately sound the S-A-M-E same. So I said, if Gabby gets some of her genius on the field, maybe it would work for us."

"You said that about me?" I know I shouldn't be, but sometimes I'm still amazed that Katy Harris is my good friend.

"I just told you I did." Katy grinned. She knew when I was fishing for a compliment.

"Oh, and Coach Raddock said we need to do something special for your last talent squad meeting, when you're ready," Katy said.

"You told Coach Raddock I was moving?"

"I said maybe moving."

As nutty as it sounds, the more my friends all thought I couldn't do this, the more I knew I had to. That I **WOULD**. Wasn't the true test of a star athlete playing in even the toughest conditions and when no one believed in her and then **WINNING AGAINST THE ODDS**?

There I went, thinking about winning again. But sometimes it was win or perish. Like that movie with Indiana Jones, a kind of crabby man with a hat. My dad watches it all the time and goes as Indiana Jones every Halloween. But in one scene, Indiana Jones is running away from this giant boulder that's rolled out of some cave. The rolling boulder for me is moving to Seattle, and the All-Pros Play is my desperate run to avoid it. If Indiana Jones can avoid being smooshed by his big rock, why can't I? Rocks don't always win!

"What are your talents?" I asked the newbies, dodging all talk of the move.

The sixth graders must have still not been used to eighth graders talking to them, because most of them mumbled responses I couldn't understand. Katy spoke up again. "We've got Eric, who does modern dance. Meekayll is a writer, Tessa can juggle, and Aasma does art installations using homemade slime."

"Wow," I said. "It's going to be pretty awesome to compete with you all in the talent showcase."

"Are you the poet Katy told us about?" Aasma asked.

"Are you the girl who's running for class president, with the poster that says . . . ," Eric began.

"Gabby's got your back? Gabby's a home run? Gabby Garcia has her thinking cap on . . . . **FOR YOU**?" I rattled off several of my better slogans.

"Yeah, those," Eric said. "But Katy said you might move. So how can you be president?" Why were people overlooking my excellent platform to gossip about something I wasn't going to let happen?

"I'm voting for her," came another voice. It was Rachel, the sixth-grade girl I'd talked to about my plan for athletic opportunities. She sat on the bleachers next to Tessa. "I thought her ideas were weird at first but she **DID** take the time to talk to me, and every other candidate just shoved a flyer in my face. Or didn't even care I had a face."

"Thanks for that, Rachel . . ."

"You convinced me to branch out," she added.

"What's your talent?" I asked her.

"Not sure yet, but I'm riding along with the squad until something surfaces."

I liked Rachel. And if I could inspire *her*, wouldn't I do even more good inspiring the *whole school*? It was as if everything was going my way. Except for the Seattle prospect. And my busted arm. And my friends trying to celebrate me so they could send me away. I guess my grades could be better. But everything else was going my way!

I wasn't going to run from the boulder, like crabby Indiana Jones; I was going to hoist it up and pitch it far, far away from me. And then make sure it never rolled back into my life.

"I'll be sticking around, so don't believe the hype," I said. "Well, believe the hype about me and vote! A vote for me is a vote for stability!"

If anyone had told me that I'd be this optimistic about staying in Peach Tree a week ago, I would have laughed, and then probably cried. If anyone had told me I would

feel
this way because
I had **PETER** on my side, I
would have taken their temperature and gone through a
list of all the world's other Peters
to make sure they weren't talking about my brother.

But things change fast! Just like my parents' plans to
move would change as soon as we ran the All-Pros Play.

As long as I was thinking positive, I decided to wish
Nolan Chao a good game.

CHANGE OF PLAY: SIDELINED BUT SO NECESSARY (THAT'S ME!)

I may not have had the perfect ideas in mind, but my sudden decision to be nice to Nolan felt right: getting over my feelings about him taking my place would be like hurling one chunk of the boulder, at least. Devon had pitched the last game, so it was his turn to take the mound. But when I circled around the stands to the dugout, it was Devon coming in from warm-ups.

"Where's Nolan?" I asked Coach Hollyligher.

"He's not starting," Coach said with a small frown, looking stressed. There are several kinds of coaches, and Coach Hollylighter was the calm but stern kind. Stressed was new for her. I looked at Mario, who was getting his batting gloves on.

"Where's Nolan?" I whispered.

Mario shook his head. "He was suiting up in the locker room, but then he didn't come out."

"What happened?"

Mario shook his head and looked spooked. "I don't know."

The game was starting and Devon was on the mound. I stood against the dugout fence, and my stomach dropped. All my confident thoughts were replaced with a bad feeling about the game, like stepping into a house you know is haunted. Not that Devon couldn't handle pitching today (or any day), but being put in the game because your team **COULDN'T FIND** the other pitcher wasn't going to get you off to a great start.

The first batter from Luther came to the plate, a boy named Jonathan Dominguez who'd been a year behind me in school and who was now much taller than me. A lot of the time, everyone was, but I'd specifically remembered Jonathan being shorter than me when we went to school together.

I love pitching to really tall batters. I could almost hear my mitt as I folded it in and out three times. Of course, I wasn't wearing one, but I knew the sound. I could almost feel the soft leather covering my hand. Which reminds me, I haven't given my glove its usual maintenance appointment lately.

GLOVE CARE LIST

- Brush away dirt and debris by using a brush or piece of cloth

- Use a bit of leather cleaner to ensure the dirt is really gone (nothing should get between your glove and the ball!)

- Every few weeks or games, use a glove conditioner to keep the leather soft (don't use too much; it will weigh your glove down!!)

- At least weekly, give your glove positive affirmations (suggestions: "Thanks for giving me a hand!" "You're quite a catch!" "I always have a ball with you!")

If I'd been catching (Coach Hollylighter had made me try it over the summer), I would have signaled for Devin to throw a slider, given Jonathan's height, so the ball would drop just as he swung for it. (As a rule, Coach Hollylighter likes us to go easy on sliders and curves so we don't screw up our elbows before we're fully grown, but Devon and I are careful.) Devon hurled a fastball at him, and it must have gone right toward his bat's sweet spot. He hit her first pitch into far left field, where a new Penguin (a seventh grader who'd quit lacrosse and asked

Coach for a tryout to play in the tournament) ran to get under it but couldn't in time. Jonathan made it to first, then second.

I could feel what Devon was feeling as she tried to shake off the bad start. She huffed out a breath and looked to the dugout and bullpen, probably hoping Nolan had shown up. Still no Nolan. With everyone else taking spots on the field, it meant Devon wouldn't even have a reliever this game.

The next batter stood at home plate, waiting for her pitch. It was critical Devon didn't get nervous because she'd let someone on base. Some pitchers would be totally miserable about that first batter, but she was an expert at managing her mound mood. Usually.

But she tossed a wild pitch way outside instead.

Every pitcher has bad innings, but starting your game with one is the worst. Devon needed to rest her arm, and the longer she tried to throw with it, the harder things were going to get.

"I'm going to go find Nolan," I told Coach. I stood up and tried to fold my arms across my chest with determination. Too bad the cast got in the way of that and I sort of hit myself in the throat.

"I saw him in the atrium last," Coach Hollylighter said.

In the bleachers, Diego was bent over his notebook and

Katy was chatting with the talent squad, but Johnny saw my face as I stepped out of the dugout. "Is Devon okay?" he asked me, and we looked over to see her wiping her forehead. She'd just let the second batter get a walk.

"Nolan was supposed to pitch," I said. "I think Devon is feeling the pressure."

"I wonder if the team's off balance with you not on the field," Johnny said, looking like someone who possibly had an instrument to measure this balance in his backpack. A very cute someone.

"Maybe, but they definitely are going to need someone to relieve Devon."

The Penguins needed **ME** to relieve Devon. But if I couldn't be on the mound, I had to be useful in some other way.

Nolan was still in the atrium. His mitt wasn't on his hand, or even in his lap. It was on the floor in front of him, like he'd tossed it there. Uh-oh.

"Hi," I said. I sat down in the chair next to him.

He looked frightened to have me talk to him. "Gabby Garcia," he said, like this was a bad thing. "Did Coach send you to kick me off the team?"

I shook my head. "No, I sent me. Is something wrong?"

"No," Nolan said, but he gave his tossed-aside mitt a look that said something was very wrong.

I sat there for a minute, counting down in my head and waiting. Ten, nine, eight, seven, six . . . he would tell me.

"I just . . . can't pitch." Nolan said what I thought he was going to say. A pitcher didn't get angry at his glove for nothing.

"You were great the other day," I said. "You definitely can pitch." I wanted to be nice to him, because we pitchers can be very sensitive.

"No, I mean, I **CAN'T** pitch. Like I feel like I forgot how." Nolan kicked the tile floor with the tip of his cleat and sighed really loud. "You must think I'm a weirdo."

"No, I think I know what this is."

"Are you going to tell me I don't have what it takes? Because I already know," Nolan answered before I could even say more. He was really down on himself. I never would have guessed his swagger could turn to this.

"I'm going to tell you that you have the yips," I said.

"The whats?"

I explained that the yips are what happen when you let all your worst thoughts take over and you sorta kinda forget how to play baseball and feel like you'll never remember again. "So what were you thinking about when you were getting ready for the game?"

"At first, only that I was pitching," Nolan said. "But then I started to think about this . . . . pattern I think I have. In my summer league, every time I had a good game, I would really screw up the next game. But this is Piper Bell! If I screw up here, I'll be off the team. It's like I forgot how to throw. I can't even get my glove on."

"You're one hundred percent in the yips. I hear them in your voice," I said. "Let's get to the dugout, and from there, I can help you with the rest."

He pointed to his glove like it was a lump of Dumpster's fresh dog doo. "What about **THAT**?"

"I'll carry it," I said. I picked it up like it was a baby, which Nolan seemed to appreciate.

By the time we got back to the field, Luther was up 2–0 in the fourth. Devon looked miserable on the mound, or as miserable as Devon will let herself look.

Nolan wasn't even trying to conceal his mood. He was lying on the bench, looking at the dugout roof. I sat next to him.

"So I think some of it started because I was a really good tennis player," he began.

"What?" I asked him. I thought I was going to get him to watch the game.

He was telling me his problems. Okay.

GABBY GARCIA,
DUGOUT THERAPIST

"I played tennis when I was little and I was good, and my parents play tennis and they like tennis and they **UNDERSTAND** tennis, but then when I said I wanted to do baseball, they didn't understand as much."

"And that makes you feel . . . ?" I sounded really professional.

"I feel . . . like I have to be **REALLY** great at baseball all the time to prove I made the right choice. If they could just **SEE** how great this game is for me, then it would make me feel less like the odd man out in my family."

"Hmm," I said. It sounded like Nolan was doing the same thing with baseball that I wanted to do with Peach Tree.

"See?? You don't even get it," he said. "You're **GABBY GARCIA**. You can pitch and you'll probably be class president and you don't have any problems."

I laughed. "That's not true. At all. I broke my arm by tripping over a hot dog!"

Nolan cracked up. "You **WHAT**?" Laughing is good. It upsets the yips.

As the team shuffled back to the dugout after giving up another run, everyone was surprised to see Nolan. Maybe because he was taking up the whole bench.

"Nolan's back," someone said.

"Who's up?" someone else said.

"Is he going to pitch?" Devon asked, rubbing her shoulder.

"Give us a bit; we're working through something," I said.

Madeleine went up to the plate and had a small hit that made it to center field, mostly because the Lions shortstop had missed the grab. The Penguins weren't in a flow, but at least the Lions weren't, either. After

Mario went down swinging, Ryder came up to bat and hit a solid almost-homer to left field. Madeleine scored.

"See, you don't have to play all by yourself," I told Nolan. "Your teammates are there so you don't have to get the win on your own."

He seemed to believe me, because he'd finally put his glove on. He was still tightly gripping the bench with his other hand, but it was a start.

By the seventh, with a tie score of 3–3, Devon was done. "The best way to show your parents you love baseball is to play it," I told Nolan. He looked at me like that was the right thing to say and stood up.

"Can you take over, Chao?" Coach asked. Nolan took a deep breath and nodded as he took steps out of the dugout. His strut was gone, but he was on the field.

For his first pitch, Nolan threw a fastball right down the middle. Swing and a miss. Piper Bell could stay in the tournament even if they lost to Luther, but it was better if they got the win. "I don't know how you did it, but I'm impressed, Garcia," Coach Hollylighter said. She tossed me a jersey. One with a penguin on it. "Even if you're benching it, I don't see why you shouldn't suit up."

Then Nolan flubbed. He threw a meatball to Michael Datson, who used to be a soccer player at Luther and had just switched to baseball this year. Michael wasn't very good yet, but still, his bat took a huge bite of that juicy pitch and he wound up on second. Then Nolan seemed to go for a curve when Casey Allen was at bat. (I could only think of the poem "Casey at the Bat," where the main guy is sure he'll get a hit and strikes out.) But Luther's Casey snatched a piece of it for a line drive that seemed to dodge our shortstop. Now Nolan had two people on base with a tie score. The new Luther center fielder, Avery Banks, came up to bat. On her first swing, she knocked the ball way past Madeleine in center field. The Luther fans went wild as Avery cleared the bases with an in-the-park home run. The score was 5–3, Luther.

When Nolan returned to the dugout, I tensed up. What if he was mad at me for pushing him to go out there?

I started to ask him, but he mouthed the words "Thank you."

Piper Bell lost. But Nolan didn't look too miserable.

He'd made it to the mound. That was a big deal. And I'd helped make it happen.

I was sidelined but not out of the game. I couldn't be replaced so easily.

If anyone could make the All-Pros Play work, it was me.

PROSPECTS FOR A NEW SEASON OF GABBY IN PEACH TREE: Excellent.

THE GREATS: GABRIELLE "GABBY" DOUGLAS

Born: December 31, 1995, in Newport News, Virginia

Origin story: When she was a toddler, Gabby's older sister, Arielle—a gymnast—wanted to teach her baby sister the sport she loved and started training baby Gabby, who was soon flipping off the family's furniture. It took four more years before their mom made it official by signing Gabby up for lessons.

Huge moments: In 2012, she became the first African American gymnast in Olympic history to become a gold medalist in the individual all-around competition. That year, she also won a gold medal with the US gymnastics team (and repeated the team gold in the 2016 Olympics!).

Quote: "Hard days are the best because that's when champions are made."

(Gosh, I hope so, fellow Gabby!)

Gabby Garcia

English Composition/Vocab Essay

An Essay About a Misunderstanding

By Gabby Garcia

If I've learned anything in life, it's that communication is critical.
There are multiple kinds of communication, from spoken to
written to telepathic thoughts to knowing enough about a person
that you get their meaning, even when they don't specifically
articulate it.

Recently, my best friends (and one person who is sort of my
boyfriend but for the sake of this essay, let's lump him in with
friends) have misunderstood me. My family might be making a
change. I don't want to reveal the specifics, so let's say my family
plans to adopt a pet. The pet is a species I'm truly allergic to, that I
believe caused a number of physical symptoms that have **hampered**
my athletic **aptitude**.

I was counting on my friends to **comprehend** that there is no
way I will allow our family to take on this pet, which would not only
be a bad pet for me, but would also require life changes that would
keep me from seeing my friends on a regular basis. My friends
should understand that I will find a way to keep this pet out of my
life because in the past, I've always had a plan. In fact, having a plan
to address any life situation is a trait I always **embody**.

However, I'm feeling misunderstood, because instead of

129

believing I can fix this situation, my friends are celebrating my still-petless status by taking me to many places I can only go as long as this horrible **PET** doesn't enter my life. Yesterday, one of my friends (the one I'd **classify** as a boyfriend) made a big deal out of all of us going to get frozen yogurt. Even though frozen yogurt is an acceptable **alternative** to ice cream, it's really only **exceptional** for the topping options. He **alluded** to the frozen yogurt **proprietor** that I might soon be unable to visit due to the arrival of the pet.

If the frozen yogurt outing had been just a random Wednesday event, I could live with that. But my friends decided to act very **solemn**, like this was our last-ever trip to a really **commonplace** frozen yogurt **emporium**. Even as I made **counterpoints** to let them know that I was making efforts to keep a pet out of my life, and that we'd be able to enjoy frozen yogurt on future **occasions**, they seemed **resigned** to the idea that I wouldn't be able to change anything.

In conclusion, sometimes you can be misunderstood even when you believe you are clearly communicating your message. To solve this misunderstanding, I will do everything I can to prove this pet is a **BAD IDEA** for my family, which will **demonstrate** to my friends that they shouldn't have doubted me. These actions will **utilize** all my communication skills.

THE SWEET SPOT

Goal: Agree with Peter on the key points of interest for the All-Pros Play

Action: Hmm, maybe accept that Peter and I are a **TEAM**?

Post-Day Analysis:
September 14

Life has this way of moving even faster when you want it to go slower. This is different than sports, where you can call for a time-out and the action stops while you sort things out. The game cuts to a commercial while the players meet on the mound (or in a huddle or near the Gatorade).

It shows how great sports are because, even though they have their own rules, when you're in a game, the rules of life and time and space become a little flexible.

My up day at the game had come crashing down today for a few reasons. First, my dad and Louie were not even trying to hide they were researching school districts in Seattle, "just in case."

And my friends had put together another commemorative outing to mini golf, like my move was inevitable. Plus, Johnny had sent this text before school today:

> Not to worry you but polls show that students wouldn't want to vote for someone who might move. ☹

Why the sad face? Why is Johnny even asking poll questions like that? And my friends seem to want to be extra careful about my feelings—especially Johnny—but everything makes him worry, and I don't want to be the person people worry about. On the other hand, he's still working on my campaign even though he thinks I might be leaving.

What does **THAT** mean?

And why can't my friends treat me normally? And by normal, I mean Gabby Normal. A normal where I'm not going to quit until my parents stop looking at new houses and we stay here and everything is **FINE**.

Better than fine! I'm going to live in Peach Tree until I eventually go on to college and major league greatness. **AS. PLANNED.**

I guess, though, there are a few not-normal things. Like my preelection speech: I'm writing a draft of it now using all the data Johnny keeps gathering. He just sent me a text update before English class. So, right now, I'm pretending to write about the themes in *The Watsons Go to Birmingham—1963*. It's a really good book, but I can't focus on my essay.

Johnny's text:

> Meatless Mondays (strong support, as long as one of the options is veggie pizza)
>
> Squishy-chair corner in some classrooms (mostly favorable but doubts u can get $$)
>
> Ping-pong table in cafeteria (big win and staff likes it too)
>
> New student mentor program (SOLID YES, 90%!)

So the student body loves my ideas, but I can't stop thinking about how voters said they worry about electing someone who might move. And Cassie Jacobs has made me maybe moving one of her campaign issues. (Plus, polls show voters admire her smooth hair, which I cannot compete with.) Worrying about letting down voters puts even more pressure on the All-Pros Play working.

And what if the All-Pros Play should have been a solo operation? Like, why am I so nervous to tell my friends that I've drafted Peter to help? I know part of it is that after telling them all that Peter's a total nuisance, I can't throw them a curve and announce we're a sibling team. But I'm worried it's something else.

Like, what if the play goes awful and he backs out, or tattles on me? There was a moment this morning that made me wonder if he would. I couldn't find my favorite pen and it turned up next to his homework. "Can you not take my stuff?" I snapped. Then, when I grabbed two of Dad's chocolate chip cookies for my lunch, Peter said, "You've had more than me, no fair. And everyone knows the youngest gets the last cookies."

"That doesn't even make sense. Also, I called the last pack of fruit snacks and I know they didn't just disappear," I reminded him. "So these are mine."

"Your cast smells like rotten eggs."

"Your face *looks* like rotten eggs."

We were in each other's faces and I was so close to saying, "Forget the All-Pros Play," but I took a deep breath and saw Peter's expression. He looked angry. But as we stared each other down, his face changed. Even though he's as tall as me, he looked small . . . and worried. Worried like Nolan had been when he thought he was getting kicked off the team. Peter and I had a small case of the yips. Or one yip.

So as we left the house for our different schools, I said, even though I didn't want to, "Sorry for this morning." And he said, "Me too." I think it was the first real apology we'd ever made to each other.

"Meeting tonight?" I asked and he said, "Sounds great!" with relief. I felt relief, too.

We said it quietly, because we were still in **COVERT OPS** mode and we couldn't say anything to terrify Dad and Louie.

But I'm still nervous (and now sneakily writing this in geometry). We've never gotten along, and if he gets even a **LITTLE** annoyed with me, what if he turns on me, or worse, suddenly **WANTS** to go to Seattle?

He wouldn't though, right? Peter understood better than anyone else what

I was going through, and he believed in the plan. (Unlike Katy when I said at lunch that a for-sure Peach Tree Sweet Spot for Louie and Dad was the church where they got married. She said, "But won't your dad and Louie like finding new sweet spots in Seattle?" Which I'd thought of, but it was like a baseball bat: just because you *could* find a sweet spot on a new one didn't mean it was a good replacement for the bat you'd hit with for years.)

Anyway, I hope Peter believes in the plan more than that.

(Later, post–Peter meeting)

I was wrong to worry. Peter and I are **DEFINITELY ON THE SAME PAGE**. Here's the highlight reel:

As Dad made dinner, Peter and I both said we had homework to do in our rooms. (We did: we were working on staying in our **HOME**town of Peach Tree.) Peter had written his ideas out on a small pad of paper. I had mine in a school folder. (I'd have written them here, Playbook, but I'm not ready to show Peter **ALL** my secrets.)

"I hereby call the first meeting of the All-Pros Stay-in-Peach-Tree Play," I said, to make things official.

"Operation Sweet Spot is in effect," Peter said.

"That's a good name for this phase," I said.

"You came up with it . . . when you were muttering to yourself."

I wanted to correct him, but I stopped myself.

Some ideas were no-go:

Peter's idea to get a stray dog to follow us home and make it impossible to leave had holes in it. "Even if we kept the dog, we could technically bring it to Seattle," I said.

My idea to have us win the lottery so that Dad and Louie wouldn't have to work anymore had a lot of flaws. They both liked working, and millions of dollars meant they might decide to move somewhere even weirder. Like a dusty castle. Or an ocean liner. I couldn't really imagine them wanting that, but money changes people. Or so I've heard.

BECOMING MILLIONAIRE$ COULD BACKFIRE ☹

It was equally unlikely we could convince our parents that all of Seattle was haunted (Peter's idea), or to realistically fake a rain allergy (my idea, unworkable because we have rain here, too), or even to buy time by attempting to say our school years wouldn't translate over to the Seattle school system (I thought of this because it sounded official and parent-y but I really didn't know how to go about it and the paperwork would have probably been awful).

Peter also brought up an idea inspired by one of his favorite books, where two kids run away and live overnight in the Met, an art museum in New York City. I definitely liked the idea for its weirdness and surprised myself by asking him if I could borrow the book. For a plan, it seemed unrealistic, though. "First off, our parents would definitely look for us," I said.

"And find us," Peter added.

Second, it was one thing to convince Dad and Louie that Seattle was a bad idea, and it was another thing to run away. "I don't think it's fair to make them feel like bad parents," I said.

"Okay . . . well, we could just make them feel really bad about the move," Peter offered. "By not hiding how incredibly sad we are about even the idea of moving." He had a point, but I'd dismissed the Excessive Mope tactic from the get-go.

"If we do that, we'll feel bad that they stayed just because of us," I said. "If we **KNOW** it's better here, then we just need to make them see it."

Peter sat in my desk chair, which normally would have been an **OFF-LIMITS** situation, but I was surprisingly okay with it. He spun around and I gritted my teeth so I wouldn't yell, "No spinning!" I took some deep breaths instead.

"Our ideas are bad, aren't they?" he said. His face had all the signs of someone who wanted to give up. I'd seen it on teammates before, when we were down a few runs and, every time we tried to rally, we just couldn't make it on the scoreboard.

Often, in those games, players wanted to make a big thing happen, and when it didn't, it was a huge letdown. If Peter was let down, he might quit on me.

I slumped on the bed with my busted arm on my stomach. Even though I didn't need my arm to come up with a way to stay in Peach Tree, the cast even made my brain feel out of commission. We'd barely gotten started on the All-Pros Play and we were already losing!

That was it! We'd barely gotten started.

"Our ideas aren't bad, they're **WARM-UPS**," I said, suddenly inspired and sitting up. Before any game, warm-ups didn't just get your muscles working, they cleared out all the gunk that might screw you up when it was time to play.

"Like we had to stretch our brains before the real stuff?" I was impressed that Peter really seemed to get my athletic line of thinking. Had we had this much in common all along?

"Yep," I said. "And we're way off base. Remember, we have to think of things in Peach Tree that make it better than Seattle. What are some things that happen here and make it **HOME**? That's our edge."

It took us only two minutes of drumming our fingers (Peter) and aggressive doodling (me) to land on an idea: "We use **GRANDMA**," Peter said, with a glint in his eye.

"I was thinking the same thing!"

THE GRANNY NEVER LET YOU GO

Goal: Show Dad that there's nothing like a mother's love (or a mother's guilt trip) and no way you can move thousands of miles away!

Action: Leverage Grandma Garcia's total sure-to-be shock about the possible move

Post-Day Analysis:
September 15

All the elements of the play were in my and Peter's favor:

We had home-field advantage. Grandma was coming into town for the Peach Tree Fall Festival, hands down her favorite event of the year. So we'd be operating **IN PERSON**.

We had a size advantage, meaning we'd each grown a few inches (okay, Peter more than me), guaranteeing a Grandma-heartstrings win ("You're getting too big!"), meaning we couldn't move away and **GROW MORE** without her around.

We had a surprise advantage—Dad hadn't told Grandma yet. He didn't know we knew this. He was talking to Louie in the kitchen last night and Peter had gone downstairs to get his math textbook and overheard them. "Dad's worried," he told me. "Because he hasn't said anything about maybe moving to Grandma yet. So that's the whole point of her visit, kind of. That's good, right?"

"Yeah, it means we can act like she knows and she'll totally freak out and tell him he can't go!"

Then, things got even better this morning, when Grandma arrived.

"Look at these kids! So big! I need to take them out and about with me before they're embarrassed to be seen with an old lady," she said, even though no one thinks my grandma looks old. She calls herself a "snazzy senior," and she wears high-tops, like me.

Salma Garcia, aka Grandma or Abuelita

Age: Whatever she says it is

Height: 5'1" but looks taller due to wisdom

Build: Petite, but with surprising hug strength

Sport: She's the Dade County Senior Club's leading billiards player

Excels at: Being your number one fan. Also, tough corner shots at the pool table.

Motto: "How are you going to know if you can't until you see if you CAN?" —said by HER

So, there we were on a perfect Peach Tree day, at the Fall Festival. Grandma was humming a tune as she browsed each stall. She liked to look at all the crafty handmade things and ask the vendors about their techniques and inspiration and even though she never bought anything—"I have seventy-four years of stuff! I can't fit any more!"—she always

143

made the people she talked to happy because she was so interested, plus she had the Grandma Effect. It seemed like every time she was deep in conversation with a crafter, customers were drawn to the booth.

"And then you paint each little expression onto the doll's face?" Grandma was asking a man about his dolls with turning heads that each displayed a different emotion. Incredibly creepy heads and horrifying emotions, if you ask me.

He launched into the details, and Peter nudged me. "When are we gonna do it?"

"Give it time," I whispered. "We're building a comfortable lead."

We put in guesses for the contests the festival held each year: weight-guessing contests for the Bennington Farm Pumpkin Patch's biggest pumpkin and the High Peach Farm's biggest peach. Then, we got lunch at Fuzzy Fusion, where every dish featured a peach in the ingredients.

I have to say, in all the years Grandma had taken us to the Fall Festival, Peter and I had never been on better behavior. We even posed for silly photos at the petting zoo and the Peachy Keen photo display (where you stick your face in a hole so you look like a peach with legs) and no two kids had ever looked so angelic as we did, except for maybe some sleeping babies.

There was no way Grandma was going to let us move so far away. She'd let someone borrow her pool cue first (and she has a very superstitious rule that no one can touch her pool cue).

"So what's new with you kids?" she asked, picking up a triangle of her peach-and-pepper-jack quesadilla when we finally sat down to eat.

I chewed my peach-and-honey pizza slice and then said, trying to make it seem like something she already knew, "Well, Dad's news, of course."

"It's family news, really," Peter said in a stroke of brilliance, as he ate his plain grilled cheese. No peaches for him. He's a picky eater, but today I stopped myself from teasing him about his completely unadventurous palate.

Grandma tilted her head at us. "What news? Oh, you mean the book project he helped on. Turned that one in in the nick of time. Your father has always been a procrastinator."

"Oh, no, it's related to the book, though the writer he edited for, his friend LaKesha, put him up for a job . . . ," I started, sounding extremely innocent, like we weren't spilling my dad's secret news.

". . . A job in Seattle, for the paper," Peter added. "So we'd move. Didn't he tell you?" If I'd been a runner on third, he'd have driven me in with a home run.

Grandma put down her nibbled-on quesadilla with her mouth wide open in shock. "What? What kind of job?"

"Sports reporter," I said, and the way Grandma's eyes widened, I felt certain we had staying in Peach Tree in the bag. No one could look that **STUNNED** and not be ready to give her son a talking-to.

BINGO.

She pulled her phone from her purse and pressed a button. I looked at Peter, who looked as amazed as I felt.

She was calling Dad already! We wouldn't even have to wait until dinner.

"Juan, is that you? . . . I know I called your phone, I'm just making sure this is **MY SON**."

We couldn't hear what Dad was saying, but the way Grandma said "my son," there was no way Dad wasn't going to be in trouble. I felt a little bad for him.

People at the festival were slowing down because Grandma, on the phone, was gesturing wildly and saying,

"I can't believe you didn't tell me right away!" And, "I know it's not definite, but how long were you going to wait?"

Peter and I were sitting completely still, like if we moved, everything that was going right might suddenly go wrong. It was almost too easy, I thought. For a split second, all the little Gabbys were in my stomach doing the wave. Was it fair that Peter and I had changed things so quickly?

LITTLE GABBYS DOING The WAVE

But of course it was. Not choosing Seattle wasn't about us; it was about our family.

Then Grandma put an arm around me and squeezed as she said into the phone, "Because my son would have shared his good news with me immediately!"

She was smiling so big there wasn't the slightest chance she was suddenly going to tell Dad he couldn't leave his only mother so far away.

Wha . . . ? I thought. Good news? Wonderful? Peter looked at me wide-eyed.

"I'm so proud of you! We have to celebrate . . ." She glanced up and smiled at us but didn't notice how weak our return smiles were. "I know it's not for sure, but I have faith they're going to pick you. Why wouldn't they? You're my **TALENTED, AMAZING BABY BOY**." Then she said a whole bunch of stuff in Spanish that sounded very loving but was so fast it was better than my skills could follow.

GRANDMA WITH HER SCOLDING **"NO-NO"** FINGER ↓

She shook her head as she hung up and wriggled her patented Grandma Finger at us.

"You kids learn a lesson: don't keep big things from your parents, especially these good things! Your father thought he could surprise me, but how could I be surprised? That boy is so smart. Such a hard worker. Even when he does save things for the last minute."

I pushed away my paper plate of pizza. I was in no mood for peaches and honey.

"But even if they pick him, he still has to decide if he's going to take it," I said. "And move us all the way to Seattle."

Did she know how far it was to Seattle?

"I know," she said. "But he's been dreaming of this his whole life! And can you imagine how much he'll love being so close to that beautiful fish market???"

Peter and I exchanged a look. I knew the look and what it meant: the play was a bust. Big-time.

"Let's go, kids," Grandma said. "I think I should make your dad a cake."

So not only had the play failed; we'd also lost our best player to the other side.

Peach Tree: 1
Seattle: 2 (to the power of Grandma)

Random Haikus

Don't tell my best friend:
Wish I had binoculars
For the bird I saw.

Is my cat busy
Or is he avoiding me?
Pets are hard to read.

Since there's a cast on
My broke arm, my hair should be
Cooperative.

Also, shoelaces.
I need my shoes well-fastened
So I don't trip again

And, ugh, my pillow.
I like to put my left arm
Underneath. I can't.

Haikus are easy
enough, as long as there's not
a whole lot to say.

Complaints of more than
Seventeen syllables need
A longer poem.

Writing poetry
Makes me hungry. Sure hope there's
Something good in fridge.

Score. A cookie was
Waiting for me. They are the
grand slam of all snacks.

THE FOOD FOR THOUGHT

Goal: Use one of Dad's favorite things—food—to remind him there's no place like home

Action: Give Dad and Louie a literal taste of what they'll be missing with the perfect family outing to their favorite Peach Tree restaurant

Post-Day Analysis:
September 16

Even though the Grandma offensive hadn't worked, it ended up leading to the next move in the All-Pros Play.

Two minutes ago, I heard Peter's feet pounding up the stairs, and Koufax jumped off his spot on the bed and darted into my closet. He hates company.

I was still moping over the Grandma plan—not only

that it had failed, but also that she was yet another adult who was on board with the possible move. Meaning she was another adult who didn't seem to care what Peter and I wanted! I thought for sure she'd say to Dad, "Think of your children!" and Dad and Louie would realize they'd left out us key players. But no. The kids didn't even get a participation ribbon.

My pity party was in full swing when Peter knocked (a funny thing: since I'd made a point of saying he was welcome in my room, he actually knocked more often).

"Are you coming to quit on me?" I asked. I wouldn't blame him.

"No," he burst out. "I know what we can do! We're going to dinner tonight with Grandma!"

"Yeah, but the Granny Never Let You Go play was already a big zero," I reminded him.

"But we're going to a special restaurant that Dad loves."

"Casa de Mayo?" I said, suddenly excited.

"They almost picked Gus's Steakhouse," he said. "But I asked if we could go there instead."

"**YES!** Your think-ing reflexes are on fire!" I held up my hand for a high five, and when

HIGH-FIVE?

Peter slapped my palm, I tried to remember if we'd ever high-fived before. I didn't think so. I'd tried to teach him when he was a baby, but even back then, we had trouble connecting.

But now, Peter and I were on the same wavelength. Casa de Mayo is Dad's favorite restaurant. He loves everything about it. And the family that runs it loves everything about Dad. He wrote a feature story on it when they first opened that really bumped up their business, and the Rodriguezes have always been grateful. The restaurant is a second home to our family. A second home we wouldn't have in Seattle.

Dad has always said that someday he's going to go work in the kitchen just to learn their secrets. And the Rodriguez family promises he only needs to say the word and they'll get him an apron.

It was perfect: Casa de Mayo is part of our history. A history we don't have in Seattle. No one can show up in a totally new city and make it have history.

Anyway, here's the Casa de Mayo story: The Rodriguez family had moved here from a small town outside Mexico City, and when they opened the restaurant a few towns over from Peach Tree, they'd taken special care to replicate every detail of their old family business. They'd even had the same little workshop from their hometown make them tablecloths just like the ones at the original restaurant.

When Dad wrote the story, he had even tracked down the weavers in Mexico to interview them.

He's like a king over there. The Rodriguezes call him Mr. Food. He can't leave his food family!

THE MENU TO A PLAN:

- Be on our best behavior.

- Bring up other times we've had a great time at Casa de Mayo. **HISTORY POINTS!**

- Ensure the Rodriguezes know that Dad may take a job in Seattle. **YOU-CAN'T-LEAVE-US POINTS!**

- Dessert: Celebrate Dad with the famous dulce de leche cake. **EVERYTHING-TASTES-BETTER-IN-PEACH-TREE POINTS!**

(Time for dinner)

There's one problem: Louie and Dad suggested I bring a friend. Not just any friend. Louie suggested **JOHNNY**. Normally, this would be exciting (in a slightly nervous way), but now it's just an extra detail I really can't handle.

But I'd asked him, since Louie had said "call him" and watched while I did it. And he said yes, and what should he wear, and I blurted, "You always look really nice," and then blushed because I temporarily forgot the All-Pros Play and that Louie was watching me on the phone with her hand over her heart like this was a really sappy scene in a movie, which I guess to her it was.

"You don't have to come," I added to Johnny, because I was worried I'd be putting so much energy into the play, I'd leave him feeling awkward. Also, wasn't it rude to invite him at the last minute to a dinner where he'd meet my **WHOLE FAMILY**?

"Are you kidding? I want to go," he said. "When I saw you were calling instead of texting, I thought you were going to break up with me. So I'm really happy you asked me to dinner."

A million thoughts cruised through my head, the top one being, "I'm not going to break up with you!" followed by, "But I might move thousands of miles away from you." I couldn't say either of these things, so I croaked, "It should be fun."

As we hung up, I gathered all my focus for the plan. Peter and I looked like the kind of children parents would order in a catalog. We'd both even put on shoes without laces! And, because we were getting along, no less than three times on the drive over, Dad and Louie and Grandma each said, "Isn't this nice?" I told myself that if we could stay in Peach Tree, I would never be crabby about sitting in the backseat with Peter ever again.

And so we kept being nice. Hands in laps, eager to listen, not complaining about the ancient rock music on the radio. An umpire would have declared us definitely nice.

Our perfect sibling-dom left time for the adults to notice the beautiful foliage (grown-ups really love leaves) and to talk about how we didn't do this nearly enough. (How could we do it **AT ALL** if we left Peach Tree was where I hoped they'd go with that thought!) And Grandma turned to me in the minivan and said, "I can't wait to meet Gabby's beau." Then she said to Peter, "What? You're not going to tease your sister about her boyfriend?"

And Peter, realizing he should have done this, said, "I didn't know you were talking about her boyfriend. Does *beau* mean weirdo in French?" I gave him a secret thumbs-up, because if we'd been acting too perfect, everyone would have suspected something.

Once we arrived, I had to battle a near case of the yips because there was Johnny. And Johnny's mom, who was what Louie would call very chic. I gulped as she introduced herself to my parents and then said to me, "Gabby, I've heard so much about you." I stared into Johnny's mom's face for too long, until finally Grandma poked me.

"I, um, hi, um, it's nice to meet you," I finally said,

forever making Johnny's mom's first impression of me as "that girl who forgot how to talk."

We were saved from more awkwardness by the hostess, Maria, the oldest Rodriguez daughter, who was in high school. She saw us approaching and squealed with glee. "The Garcias! Hold on, let me get Dad!"

Mr. Rodriguez came out of the back and opened his arms extra wide to bring us all in for a huge hug. "My favorite family," he said. "I'm so glad to see you."

"It's the best restaurant in the world," Grandma said. "I can't come to Peach Tree without eating here!"

We headed to the really neat round booth tucked in the back of the restaurant, right next to a small fountain with flower petals floating in it. It's an unspoken rule that this is **OUR** booth when we come in. And there were already warm tortilla chips waiting, with two kinds of salsa and guacamole. Does anything say **"NEVER LEAVE"** like fresh chips? I don't think so.

"Remember when we came here for my sixth birthday and the mariachi band let me go to each table with them?" Peter said, making his eyes extra puppy-like so he looked younger than his almost-nine years.

I nodded encouragingly. He was breaking out the good stuff.

"Oh, Peter, you were so sweet and little," Louie said.

"I remember one let you hold his guitar and you almost tipped over." She sighed a proud mom sigh and I felt like I did when I had only one strike left to throw to win the game: this was definitely going to work out for us.

"We couldn't stop you from thinking big then, and we never will," Dad said, ruffling Peter's hair. Ooh! A wistful dad quote! The points were adding up!

"I always thought it was the neatest thing that Casa de Mayo was our Little League sponsor all those years," I said, absolutely wanting to lay everything on extra thick. "Everyone else had muffler shops or insurance agencies and we had a **FANCY** restaurant."

"That was your father's doing," Louie said and looked at Johnny to include him in her story. "Gabby's dad suggested the restaurant sponsor the team because he wanted an excuse to hold the team dinner here." She smiled and poked Dad's arm with a little grin and Dad blushed. They were being all couple-y, which would definitely work in our favor.

"Your team photos are right there with my story," Dad said, pointing across the room to the Wall of Fame, where the Rodriguezes had tons of photos hanging—photos of different local celebrities and my teams (and Peter's teams) and, in one of the biggest frames, Dad's story mounted on a red background.

Johnny got up to look at the story and when he came

back, he said to Dad, "Gabby told me you did a lot of sports-writing but I didn't know you did features, too." My dad beamed at Johnny's newspaper talk. I wanted to say, "How am I supposed to find a boyfriend **THIS** great in Seattle?" but that wasn't how this play was meant to work.

We kept going around the table, sharing all our favorite times and times that weren't as great but were funny now, like when, at age eight, I insisted I could eat a whole King Burrito that even Dad has trouble finishing. I was so stubborn about it that our entire family waited until closing when I took my very last bite (and got sick in the car).

It was a little embarrassing to have Johnny hear all of that until he said, "I once ate a whole box of Froot Loops so I could get the prize before my sister did and then threw up going down the curly slide at the park." Then he fidgeted with his tie and said, "I hope that's not too much information before dinner."

Everyone laughed and Dad said, "You fit right in!" It was like he'd read my mind: How could we leave when so many things are such a good fit?

When Mr. Rodriguez came around, he asked if we wanted the usuals: tamales for Dad, fish tacos for Louie, taquitos for Peter, sopes for me, and enchiladas for Grandma. Johnny ordered sopes, too, because he trusted my recommendation and joked he had a high probability of liking them, which I totally got because I appreciated his math humor. Dad ordered a few more dishes for the table to share, because the special that day was steak picado—"I thought I could smell it when I came in!"—which is braised beef with green peppers and bacon. Dad always overorders because he loves to bring food home. **HOME**, as in **HERE**.

Dad was in his element. "I hope someday you kids live in a place where you have a place that feels like yours." And I saw a little tear in his eye. If he was going to cry, we had this thing in the bag!

"Well, we have this one," I said, aiming to be subtle. I wasn't the best at being subtle—I'm a pitcher. What would a subtle pitch even look like?

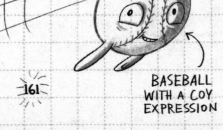

BASEBALL
WITH A COY
EXPRESSION

"We'll always have Casa de Mayo," Louie said. There was a line in one of her favorite movies *Casablanca* where the main couple said, "We'll always have Paris," but at the end they split up, so her saying that didn't necessarily make me feel good.

"Home is where you make it," Grandma said. "I mean, look at the Rodriguezes: they came so far from their home and they brought a piece of themselves to us."

I stopped with a forkful of sope halfway to my mouth and caught Peter looking stunned in his seat, too. The whole point was to get Dad and Louie to see that you couldn't have the things you loved wherever you were. You needed to **STAY** in the place that you already loved.

If Peter and I were going to win, we needed a push. Being at Dad's favorite restaurant was like being on base with two outs. We needed a batter to drive us in to score.

I got up to go to the restroom, but I took the long route. In the main dining room, the mariachi band was playing a romantic song for two older women who were holding hands, so I waited patiently. When they finally finished and left a red rose on the table, I said to the singer, "Can you please come by the big table in the back and play 'Cielito lindo'?"

The song title more or less means "Lovely Sweet One," and Dad and Louie had danced to it at their wedding.

"Of course, *chava*," he told me. "We have one more table before you."

"Okay, thank you," I said. "It's very important."

"I can tell," he said, and I felt good, like this would fix everything. Music was supposed to have all kinds of powers, right?

Satisfied, like a spy who'd found top secret information, I nodded at Peter as I slid back into the booth. He grinned and gave me a thumbs-up. "I thought you and Peter didn't get along," Johnny whispered.

"Let's just say there are new factors in that equation," I told him. He still looked puzzled but he didn't have a chance to ask more because Mr. Rodriguez came by to talk. He and Dad started to talk about the Braves making the playoffs. Then, he asked me and Peter about school and said, "Who is this?" to Johnny. Both Johnny and I started to answer at the same time, him saying, "I'm, um, we . . . she's my friend, girlfriend" and me saying, "My friend who's a boy . . . boyfriend." Mr. Rodriguez tried not to laugh. As he, Dad, Louie, and Grandma chatted, I noticed that no one mentioned that we might move to Seattle. Maybe deep down, being here with all these great memories was making Dad reconsider.

"So are we celebrating anything today?" Mr. Rodriguez asked. "Because Marta has a dulce de leche cake in back if you need help coming up with a reason to try it."

I seized my chance. "Well, Dad's up for a sportswriter job in Seattle," I blurted, hoping that Mr. Rodriguez would be shocked and horrified.

"Wow, Juan, that's . . . ," Mr. Rodriguez said.

Dad grimaced. "I'm still being considered," he said, cutting off Mr. Rodriguez, who I thought **HAD** to have been about to say, "That's an awful idea!" Dad looked at me with raised eyebrows and I knew that he was trying to say that I'd let a secret spill that I shouldn't have. But if he didn't want me to talk about his secret plans, he shouldn't have had secret plans! "I don't want to jinx it."

Even though there's nothing worse than being a jinx—a jinx can make everything go wrong, all the time—I **DID** want to jinx it. I would go through the rest of my life not being a jinx ever again if I could just jinx this **ONE THING**.

Mr. Rodriguez had left our table in a hurry, and then returned from the kitchen with his wife, Marta. She was waving her arms toward their daughter Maria and her brother Ruben, indicating they should come to our table.

I looked at Peter. Maybe the Rodriguezes were doing an intervention right now? That had to be it. They were going to gather right here at our table and put a stop to even the **IDEA** of Dad leaving. Peter's eyes bulged, like he couldn't believe our luck. Neither could I.

Maybe the intervention would involve more chips.

Mr. Rodriguez was about to say something right when the mariachis arrived. I thought about telling the band that we wouldn't need the music now, because Mr. Rodriguez and his loved ones were going to talk sense into my parents, but then I thought a little music could do nothing but good things for the moment. It would add **RESONANCE**. (Another new word from my English composition class. Really, how could Dad and Louie even consider leaving Peach Tree's excellent educational opportunities behind??)

The band launched into its song and, for real, everyone began to sing. Dad and Louie had tears in their eyes. On a lot of occasions, tears aren't ideal. For today, tears were **GREAT**. Peter and I had to adjust our faces into serious ones. We were both trying not to smile too big. Johnny leaned over and said, "I was really nervous to meet your family, but they're so nice!" And, because I felt like Peter and I were definitely on the verge of a victory, I nodded and said, "They're the **BEST**."

I couldn't believe Peter and I were going to make this work. We'd never get a trophy for it, but we'd always know that getting to stay in our hometown instead of risking a move to Seattle was firmly in our life **WIN** column.

When the band finally stopped, I held my breath, waiting for the Rodriguezes to say, "You know it's **BONKERS** to even think about a move all the way across the country when so much that you love is **RIGHT HERE**?" And then Dad and Louie would exchange a glance and nod slowly, shaking their heads like they couldn't believe they'd ever even batted the idea around. After all, the Rodriguezes were proof Peach Tree was the best place to live: they'd left a place they loved to start a life here.

But then, the Rodriguez family **CLAPPED**.

This seemed out of order; shouldn't they clap **AFTER** Dad and Louie say there's no way we're leaving?

But then, Mrs. Rodriguez gestured to the kitchen and a server came out with her dulce de leche cake on a tray. "We are so proud of you, Juan! To the start of your new journey in Seattle!"

WHAT???

"I've always said, 'That Juan Garcia is a world-class talent,' and now you are taking your talents to the world!" Mr. Rodriguez had a glass raised in a toast. Why were we toasting??? Couldn't Mr. Rodriguez see how detrimental this was to all of us? Or at least to me and Peter, who were being unwillingly dragged along on the world-class talent world tour? Shouldn't he wait to toast until he asked how **WE** felt about it?

My dad held up his hands. "This might be a little premature, because they haven't made an offer yet."

A TOAST TO OUR FAILURE!
WAY TO RUB IT IN...

Louie squeezed his arm. "But I know they will."

"They'd be loons not to!" Grandma added.

Everyone agreed to this and they all clinked and clinked and clinked again.

No one even noticed that Peter and I didn't join in.

Not even Johnny, who raised his glass, too. But he whispered, "Are you okay? You look pale."

Of course I was pale! I was very **NOT OKAY**. Also, wondering why no one seemed to care that everything was terrible. Except Peter, who slumped defeatedly in his chair.

I totally understood.

At least when you lost in a game, no one toasted your failure.

Seattle: 3
Peach Tree: 1

THE WE'VE GOT NO GAME

Goal: Rally!
Action: Put All-Pros Play temporarily on hold while Peter and I come up with a new strategy . . . but also, RALLY!

Post-Day Analysis:
September 18

Piper Bell was hanging in there in the charity tournament. Even after the loss to Luther, they were looking pretty good when I got to the field today. Or they looked good compared to how I felt, because after my double losses over the weekend, I was impressed by people willing to show up to try at anything. Even if you were doing your best, it could all be taken away from you and moved to Seattle!

But, okay, I'd shown up. So maybe I was rallying, too. There had to be a way to prove I needed to stay at Piper Bell, in Peach Tree. I just had to find it.

"Coach is pitching Nolan today," Devon muttered when I found her on the bench.

"The King Prep Royals are so good," I said, knowing exactly what Devon was thinking. She had the experience against tough teams, and yet Nolan was getting the start. I wasn't anti-Nolan anymore, but he was still new. "Is he ready?"

"Yeah, Coach says she's conserving my energy in case we need a reliever," she said. "Do you think she knows my secret? I'm starting to worry it's showing in my game."

"Huh?" I said. Devon had a secret? "What secret?"

Of course Devon had a secret. Devon probably had dozens of secrets! I tried to imagine what kind of secret would affect Devon's ability to be the starting pitcher.

POSSIBLE DEVON SECRETS

- She was part of a set of twins who were taking turns being Devon?

- She was a movie star researching a role for a baseball film?

- She was actually a thirty-five-year-old woman posing as a middle schooler?

- She had an extra index finger that gave her an unfair pitching advantage and no one had noticed it until now? (But there was no rule that said you couldn't pitch if you had extra fingers. Not one that I knew of.)

"I'll tell you later," Devon said, flexing her hand as she examined her fingers. Ugh. I wanted to know! "But I think Mario needs to talk to you. He was in the atrium when I saw him last."

Another player in the atrium, I thought. Gabby to the rescue!

MARIO SKULKING BEHIND A PLANT

...?

When I got there, Mario was in a weird spot. Like, literally a weird spot. He was hiding behind a plant. Mario is a big guy so hiding isn't really the right word for it, but he was doing his best.

"What's going on, Mario?" I asked, trying not to sneak up on him.

He peered out from behind a large leaf. "I can't go out there," he said.

"I can't carry you," I told him, holding up my arm.

"Haha," he said, not laughing. I think it's unfair to say "haha" when you don't laugh. "But I think it's something like what Nolan had . . . the yaps."

"You mean the yips?"

"Yup."

Our conversation was bound to become confusing quickly. And the team needed him on the field. So I asked, "Do you wanna talk about it?"

Mario nodded. "I think so."

Dr. Gabby, Dugout Therapist, was in session! The goal? Get Mario to the dugout. "What seems to be the problem?" Asking Mario to explain his woes felt good, mostly because they were proof that I wasn't the only one with woes.

"I'm worried about my batting," Mario said, and I did a Devon-style blink at him because I thought he had to be joking.

"Your batting? What, you're tired of hitting home runs?"

He smiled, just a little, like he was remembering his last homer. The smile quickly turned to a frown. "That's exactly it. The home runs," he said. He'd come out from behind the plant, which seemed like a positive step. A step **TOWARD** the baseball field. "What if people only see me as a home-run hitter?"

"They don't see you that way when I'm pitching!" I said. I couldn't help it.

"Very funny," Mario said. Like his "haha," the comment wasn't followed by a real laugh. Rude.

I had to be in therapist mode, though, so I nodded thoughtfully and began walking slowly toward the field, getting Mario to join me. "Do you not like hitting home runs?"

"I **LOVE** hitting home runs," he said. "But don't I need more to me than a superpowerful swing?"

He heaved a sigh and looked at me with his shoulders kind of slumped. Back when he was my opponent, I might have **WANTED** to see him look so devastated. Now that I knew him, it was terrible to see him so miserable.

"So, maybe you want to develop your game so you can develop yourself," I told him. It sounded good but even I wasn't sure what I meant.

Mario's eyes lit up. "You're a genius," he said. Then added, "What does that mean . . . develop myself?"

Darn. I had to figure that part out. We were outside the school now, walking the path toward the baseball fields. I knew if I could get him near his bat, everything would be fine. Mario was meant to be on the field, like me. "Maybe you need to be more strategic and look at the whole field. Like, you could work on your opposite-field hitting. Or maybe sometimes you could hit a sacrifice fly." (**OLD ME**, you might have forgotten some things and be asking, "Why wouldn't a batter **ALWAYS** go for a home run?" but the truth is, sluggers like Mario get more home runs than other batters but they also strike out more. If he could be more versatile, Mario could make his whole game better.)

"So, I have to reprogram myself . . . to not be so great?" He nodded seriously.

(Home-run hitters like him and great pitchers like me can be a little full of ourselves.) I was tempted to remind him he struck out plenty. Yet I couldn't, because Mario being full of himself right now was crucial to eliminate the yips.

"Maybe it's that you have to know when to be great, and when it's better to be **GOOD**," I told him as we arrived at the dugout.

Devon and Coach Hollylighter looked relieved to see Mario. "How are you feeling now, Salamida?" Coach said.

Mario took a deep breath. "Like I don't want to hide behind a plant."

"That's probably the first time anyone's said that in a dugout," Devon said.

Mario and I laughed, and I handed him his bat. "Think you can do it?"

"I hope so," Mario said. "But thanks for listening."

Mario seemed more like his old self as everyone got ready for their at bats. When he was up, I clenched my teeth, worrying the yips would attack again, but Mario tapped his bat on home plate, like usual. And he swung away, as usual. I didn't know if he'd take my advice to try some other at-bat tactics, but at least he was in the game.

Why was I able to help Nolan and Mario but not find a good next phase for staying in Peach Tree? What if my play was a loser? What if breaking my arm was a bad omen? My cast stinks. (Literally stinks.)

THINGS A CAST SMELLS LIKE AFTER A WHILE

- A sock that you wore to practice, dipped in milk, and then left in the sun

- A fishbowl that's been neglected for a long time

- That Tupperware container at the back of the fridge with an unknown origin

- A sweatshirt pocket where you've left some cheese and forgotten about it for twelve years

The Penguins took the field. Devon waited with me in the dugout while Nolan took the mound. She was staring at the field in her glinty-eyed way, and I thought maybe I could give her dugout therapy, too. Or at least find out her **SECRET**! I got up and stood next to her. "Are you going to tell me your secret?"

Devon paused. I couldn't see her face but I knew she was blinking as she decided what to say.

"I didn't tell Coach I started taking archery lessons. My arm's sore. I'm worried Coach some-how knows and that's why she didn't start me today."

"Archery?"

DEVON IN HER RENAISSANCE LOOK

"Yeah, I tried it out at a Renaissance faire and liked it and now I can't stop."

"You go to Renaissance faires?"

"Yeah, I like to dress up and enjoy a turkey leg while I watch a joust. No big deal."

Wow. These were secrets

176

on top of secrets. I would have been less surprised if Devon had been a thirty-five-year-old pseudo eighth grader.

"Well, how do you feel about this? Are you confused? Worried about what this means for you? Do you need me to help you get in tune with yourself?"

Being the team's therapist was growing on me.

"Sometimes, I feel almost too in tune with myself," Devon said. "But I'm not too worried about it. I just want to play."

I should have known Devon wouldn't need my help. We turned back to the game to see how Nolan looked on the mound. His parents were in the crowd today, and Nolan seemed calm about it. His first few innings were a little uneven—he struck out some of the Royals' better players, but he let a few batters that could have been easy outs get by. Still, he didn't seem in danger of a case of the yips.

Mario's case of them was making a return, though. He struck out in his next at bat, but not because he was swinging—he let three great pitches pass him by! Later, on first base, he missed one of Nolan's throws because he seemed deep in thought.

By the ninth, we were down by two, 6–4. Then, Nolan nailed a line drive to center that brought Ruby Garland and Tommy Aiello in for runs. A tie score, 6–6. Nolan was on second. Ryder Mills was on third. We only needed Ryder to score to get the win. Otherwise, we'd go to extra innings. Mario was up.

"He's due for a homer," Devon said.

"All we need is one run," I said. "Not a whole homer." I didn't tell her that I'd told Mario not to go for homers.

Devon chuckled. "Like Mario would ever not try for the homer," she said. "It's who he is."

Maybe she was right, and it was too hard for Mario to take his swing down a notch. My stomach clenched. What if my advice to Mario ruined the game?

MARIO, WHO CAN'T IMAGINE HIMSELF BEING **LESS GREAT** AT BASEBALL

Mario took a few practice swings and walked to the plate. He was doing everything more slowly than usual, and he didn't get into his stance right away. On the first two pitches, he swung huge, and the ball blew right by his bat.

"We're going to go into extra innings," Coach Hollylighter said. "DeWitt, I think Nolan needs some relief out there."

Devon started to get ready to go to the bull pen, but she whispered to me, "Sure, I have to go in when all the pressure's on."

Until Mario did something very un-Mario. On the next pitch, he slid his hand down the bat and just barely tapped the ball.

Mario bunted!

A perfect bunt that plopped itself down midway between the pitcher and the catcher. An even more perfect bunt because it was the most surprising thing a batter like Mario could do. The pitcher was so confused, it took her a second to remember to go get the ball as the catcher covered home. Ryder, who must also have been surprised, was charging for home plate, trying to beat the throw.

I wasn't breathing—a squeeze play can do that to you—but Ryder slid into home just before the ball hit the catcher's glove. He'd scored! We'd won!

"I can't believe he **BUNTED**," I said.

"I know. One more game and then we'll be in it for the trophy," Devon said.

The tournament was almost over? My stomach jumped. I needed a bunt-level surprise for the All-Pros Play before my Peach Tree life was over, too.

THE MOJO MISSION

Goal: Get back on track to find the Peach Tree sweet spot
Action: Remove extra worries and focus

Midday Analysis:
September 20

When a coach or a star player promises his or her team they'll be winners and then it doesn't work out, I wonder if the coach or player hides out from their team because they feel lousy about failing to deliver on their promise.

I was definitely doing that with Peter. This morning at breakfast, while Dad and Louie were in the other room, Peter had caught my eye and said, "Have you thought of anything?"

"I'm working on it, but I can't talk about it now," I lied, even though I had **ZILCH. NOTHING. NADA.** Then, hoping he was asking because **HE** had a great idea, I said, "What about you? Any new ideas?"

Peter stirred his cornflakes. He likes to make them as mushy as possible before he eats them. It drives me nuts. "No," he said. He wasn't lying to me, which only made my lie feel worse.

"I'll fill you in later," I told him and was relieved when Louie came into the kitchen, meaning I had to stop making promises to him I didn't know if I could keep.

I had no time to think about the All-Pros Play at school because Katy had called an emergency meeting of the talent squad so that I could rehearse my president speech. I spent most of my classes scrawling notes (I've gotten better writing with my right hand but I'm still messy!) of what I wanted to say. Nothing I wrote was working. None of it had pizzazz. I even tried writing a presidential poem.

The thing was, I felt more and more like I was going to move and shouldn't be giving this speech. Maybe Yogi Berra was wrong and things *were* over before they were over.

It didn't help that Katy seemed to think I was right about that. "Whoa, this could be the grand finale of your talent squad life," she said when I got to the auditorium, which she'd reserved for so-called official business. "The squad is going to be poetless."

I almost told her not to worry, like a reflex. But I **WAS** worried. After weeks of telling my friends I was going to figure this out, I hadn't!

So instead I said, "I'm really not ready to give a speech." It was the truth.

"We'll help you," Katy said. "They don't call us the talent squad for nothing."

I wanted to ask **WHY** she was saying two totally different things—a. that this could be my last talent squad meeting; but b. that she'd help with a speech to make me president of a school I wouldn't be going to.

To add to the mixed signals, Johnny arrived with more notes and stats. "The students really like your informal style," he said. "So don't make your speech too speech-y. And don't bring up that you might move."

SEE?

"That won't be a problem," I said and showed him my pages of crossed-out ideas. "This doesn't even resemble a speech."

I stood behind the podium and looked at the small cluster of talent-squadders. I read my scribbles as I tried to think of something to say.

I started, "Hi, my name is Gabby Garcia and I've had

the honor of talking to some of you over these past few weeks." I realized I sounded like someone who was about to resign, not run for president.

"I can't hear you," said Rachel, the new talent-squadder.

"Speak up!" That was Arlo Cole, a champion speech-maker.

I projected my voice as best as I could into the microphone, but it was flat. As I looked out over the faces of the talent squad, and Johnny and Katy, I didn't think I could leave them. But I couldn't **LEAD** them, either. Running for president was a big deal, and so was the All-Pros Play. I was a **GABBY DIVIDED**.

I stepped off the stage. Then I did something sort of bunt-like: I handed the mic to Johnny.

He looked at it. "Is there something wrong with the mic?"

I shook my head and then, remembering Mario's play and how it showed that game winning didn't mean you always got to be the big star, I said, "I know I started the campaign, but you should be the one to finish it."

The talent squad gasped. Arnold Kapoor, an actor who loved all things drama, said, **"OH. MY. GOD. WHAT IS HAPPENING?"**

Johnny looked at me with the same kind of expression. Although his was less astounded and more concerned.

I said, "Think about it. You know the issues and you know the students and you **CARE**."

"But my polls show . . ."

I looked him in the eye. "Exactly! Your polls! You know this stuff. And you've been doing a lot of the work."

Johnny looked at his feet. "It's easy to do the work when there's a candidate I believe in," he said. "I like doing the data for someone I want to vote for."

"Awww," said Grace Chang, the talent squad's resident street artist (and lover of romance novels). She was totally right. "Aww" was exactly what I was thinking. But there was no time for heart-eyes; I had to convince Johnny.

"And I want to vote for you," I told him.

The entire talent squad was watching us like we were characters on a soap opera.

THE TALENT SQUAD
=SHOCKED=

"This is really adorable and inspiring, but also I have some illusions I need to work on, so can we wrap it up?" Lisa Clover said.

"Shh!" Sophia Rodriguez told her.

"You have my vote," Rachel said to Johnny. "If Gabby endorses you, that's enough for me."

I had a fan. Johnny looked at his clipboard and then at me. "Did you find out you're for sure going to move or something?"

"Yeah, is there something you're not telling us?" Katy was giving the kind of stern look I thought only moms could do.

"**NO**," I said. "But I don't think now is a good time to run for office." **NOT** running would give me more time to figure out how to stay in Peach Tree, was what I didn't tell them.

"I don't have a chance," Johnny said. "I haven't made any posters and Piper Bell has never elected a boy."

"There's a first time for everything," Katy and I said at the same time. Then Katy gave me a long look. "But you were really into this, Gabs. Are you sure you want to give it up?"

I didn't want to give anything in my life up. Especially being president. But, because of everything else, my heart wasn't in giving speeches and shaking hands and being a great candidate. It wasn't right to run if I was only sort of jogging.

"I don't, but I should," I said. "I need to sacrifice something."

And then, a **PLAY** came into my head.

THE YOU'RE-RUINING-MY-LIFE SACRIFICE

Goal: Make my parents realize how they are derailing my entire life!

Action: Give up my presidential run (**CHECK!**) and blame the possible move to Seattle

Post-Day Analysis:
September 20 (cont'd)

Peter looked as glum before dinner as he had during break-fast. He was on the couch with our cat, Koufax, and kicking a hacky sack from foot to foot slowly. When I burst in the room, he perked up immediately.

"You have an idea," he said. "I can tell."

He kicked the hacky sack too hard and it flew across the room, but I was glad he was excited. "I know we said we didn't want to whine and scream and throw tantrums and we had to make the Peach Tree and Seattle decision feel like **THEIR** idea, but this idea is sort of halfway between that."

"A compromise," Peter said.

"Sort of." I told him about the talent squad meeting, and what had happened, and what I'd figured out.

At dinner, we put our plan in motion.

"Have you heard anything from the paper?" Peter, eating a plain cheese quesadilla, asked Dad, who was plating my and Louie's quesadillas, both filled with shrimp and sweet peppers. "I was just wondering because Justin might have a sleepover for his birthday next month and I don't know if we'll be here."

Dad looked to Louie and then to us. "I think they're down to the final round," Dad said. "But even if I get the job, we'll probably still be in town for Justin's party."

"Oh, okay," Peter said. We'd been hoping he'd get the runaround on the answer, showing how unfair it is that we can't even make plans. Point for our parents.

We dug in to dinner, waiting before I launched Phase Two.

"What's new at school?" Louie said. It was an everyday question that could have had an everyday answer. But I had to play my answer today for all it was worth. Or, really, all the parental guilt it could cause.

"I practiced my speech for the president race," I said. "It went really well." The success of the play came by unfolding things slowly.

"Oh, that's great, honey," Dad said. "When's the election?"

"Next week," I said. "But it doesn't matter. I realized I needed to drop out." There. I'd said it. Now, I needed them to swing at my pitch.

Here was Louie, stepping in like I'd put the ball just where she wanted it. "Why did you decide that?"

Telling them felt like cheating. It was like a pitcher putting weird stuff on the ball to get a better grip for throwing fancy pitches (by making it sticky) or to throw faster (by making the ball slicker).

WEIRD STUFF PITCHERS HAVE PUT ON THE BALL TO CHANGE THEIR PITCHES

- Pine tar
- Sunscreen (good for faces, not for the ball!)
- Vaseline
- Spit

- Boogers (picking your nose on a baseball field should be against the rules)

- Earwax (gross and unsanitary)

"Because we might move," I said, glancing at Peter to see if I was doing a good job. He hid a smile behind his quesadilla triangle. "I had a good shot but it would be wrong to win and have to leave."

"Wow," Dad said, putting his fork down. This was **SERIOUS**. "That's a big decision."

"Definitely," Louie agreed.

"I was running a really good campaign," I said—definitely adding a lot of extra gunk to my Parent Guilt ball. "But I guess it's what I have to do."

"It's not like you would have won, anyway," Peter said. We'd agreed he had to say something a little nasty to sell the play.

"This is a big sacrifice, Peter," Louie said, frowning at him. She reached to squeeze my hand. Mom sympathy! Giant points!

"It is," Dad added. "It's really not very fair to Gabby. I feel terrible." Dad sympathy! A parental guilt double play! Where were the fireworks? We needed to show a replay on the Jumbotron, at least.

"I wish there were something we could do," Louie said.

There was! All they had to do was say: "We can't move!" Of course, now that Johnny was in the race I wasn't going to tell him to quit, but I'd handle that later. I'd be staying in Peach Tree so I'd have **PLENTY OF TIME** for future presidential runs.

Dad smiled at me. "I hear Seattle can be a great place for young world changers."

"For sure, it's such a civic-minded place," Louie said, suddenly brightening. "You'll be great! Let's just hope we wind up there!"

What? This was worse than letting a batter get a home run off me. This was the ball exploding my hand.

Or it hurt that much, at least.

I tried to smile, even as my eyes got itchy like they wanted to cry. I couldn't look at Peter, who I knew would be looking at me like I was the pitcher who lost the game. I didn't want to change the world if my whole world was going to be completely different.

Seattle: 3
Peach Tree: 1 (and in a major slump!)

THE SHOW HIM HE'S BOSS
(HE IS!)

Goal: Show Dad he's really valued in the community at large

Action: Enter a winning application in the Community Alliance Citizen of the Year Award

Post-Day Analysis:
September 21

Like a rookie player who steps off the bench and drives in a winning home run, it was Diego who helped Peter and me come up with our next Stay in Peach Tree play.

True, after the failures of the Granny Never Let You Go and the Food for Thought, Peter and I both wanted to throw in the towel. And after yesterday's sacrifice had failed to score, we felt even more defeated. When I finally got the courage to talk to him last night, Peter wasn't upset with me. He was mad at Dad and Louie. "It's so wrong that they don't even care how awful this is."

He was talking like he had more faith in me than ever. As he'd put it, "That was a huge play. Even if they didn't change their minds, they definitely felt guilty. Sometimes in soccer, you don't get to score but you wear down the other team." It was kind of nice that even if we spoke different sports languages, we still understood each other.

One plus today was my visit with Dr. Phillips. She said she couldn't do anything about the cast smell but assured me my arm was healing better than expected and I'd be able to be active right away once the cast came off. That had me energized, so I called on Peter to regroup in my room.

I stocked my room with snacks to supercharge Peter and me. After ten minutes, the snacks were gone and we had absolutely zero useful ideas. We kept going over our last few plays, looking for places we could have done better. "It was like everything was going our way, and then it wasn't," Peter said of the Casa de Mayo incident, groaning.

"I know. I thought we had it in the bag when the mariachis came to our table and then suddenly I felt like I needed a bag . . . to barf in."

We were acting like a baseball team that kept torturing itself by watching the game where we'd lost the World

Series. "This isn't good for us," I said. "We'll never think of anything if we can't stop watching our blooper reel."

Then a text came from Diego:

> At Luther, taking yearbook photos on baseball field. U should stop by.

Ugh. On one hand, I did want to go, because I felt cooped up in my room and thought the walk would be good to jog my brain. Still, I dreaded seeing Diego at the field of our old school. What if this was some new trip down memory lane? Too depressing.

Maybe it didn't have to be. Before I even realized I was doing it, I invited Peter to go with. "Uh, now?" he said. "We're in the middle of a strategy session."

I pointed to the empty bags of licorice and popcorn. "We're in the middle of a stress-eating session. We need to get out," I said, using all the Team Leader energy I had.

When I showed up with Peter, Diego looked at me like I'd shown up pulling a gorilla in a wagon. He sounded alarmed and said, "Did something happen?"

"What would have happened?" I asked.

"Like a family emergency, or some other weird thing that forced you to bring Peter along. Is he hurt?" Diego squinted at Peter, maybe looking for parts of him that were gauzed or bandaged.

"No, I wanted to come," Peter said.

Diego looked more stunned than if one of the birds he was fond of watching stopped tweeting to tell him it needed some privacy. (Question for later: Do birds get annoyed by bird-watchers, spying on their bird lives and bird ways?)

INVASIONS OF BIRD PRIVACY:

DURING MEALTIME

IN THE BIRDBATH

THIS IS A PRIVATE REHEARSAL!

WHILE WORKING ON THEIR MUSIC

"Did you bump your head?" Diego asked him.

"Dad had a freelance, office, call-type thing," I fumbled. "He needed some quiet at home so he asked if Peter could tag along."

I didn't want to get into the exact reasons Peter and I were together. My friends didn't get the All-Pros Play, and they'd get it even less if I told them I'd been teaming up with Peter, even if he's the only person who believes this can work, and . . . I don't think I can do it without him.

Whoa. Weird.

Diego still looked quizzical, but I changed the subject and said, "Wow, look at the old field."

It had been a while since I'd seen the ballfield at Luther. Actually, the last time I'd seen it was in April when I'd pitched my last game as a Luther Lion. That game—where I'd been throwing a no-hitter—was stopped mid-inning because Luther had to close after a hazmat crew found asbestos inside it.

I had thought my life was over that day. And then I'd gotten transferred to Piper Bell and started fresh but fresh hadn't been very fresh at all. It had been so awful that even after I forced my way onto the baseball team, I'd quit the team—something I'd never thought I'd do. I became a field hockey player! Or, really, a talent squad member. I'd started writing poetry! That day when my life at Luther ended had been one of the worst days ever, but somehow, I'd created a whole new version of me that I was pretty happy with. I had new friends, a newfound talent, and even a boyfriend (I think).

It's funny, Playbook, but if Asbestos Day had never happened, you wouldn't be here. *I* wouldn't be here. Like, *I* would be here, but not in the same way I'm here now: not Gabby Garcia, Piper Bell student, with friends I didn't know existed before.

Bob: *Is it just me, or is Gabby getting a touch philosophical, Judy?*

Judy: *Every great athlete is more than who you see on the field, don't you think?*

Bob: *Sure. I suppose it makes sense that Gabby's flexing her mental muscles since she's still in a cast.*

Judy: *The question is, what is Gabby driving at here?*

Judy was right: Was I imagining that a Seattle version of me might end up as happy as the post-asbestos Piper Bell, talent-squad-joining, poetry-writing, boyfriend-having version, was now (because, even with a broken arm, I *am* happy, except for the part where I might move to Seattle)?

I believe a person can be lucky, but I couldn't imagine Seattle version of Gabby would wind up as happy as I was now. "Lightning doesn't strike twice."

"What did you just say?" Diego asked, and I realized I'd said that lightning thing out loud. Oops.

"Oh, I said that the new scoreboard looks nice," I bluffed. It actually did. When I'd played there, it was made of wood and faded and cracked, but now it was replaced with a new electronic scoreboard that said "Home of the Luther Lions" across the top and "Let's Roar!" along the bottom.

"You're right, I should get that in the frame," Diego said and snapped a few photos of the kids in the outfield. While he did, I gave Peter a look and whispered, "Make sure you don't act too nice to me! Diego can't know we're working together. He might accidentally blurt something to his mom and she'll tell Louie and then we're doomed!"

"You're right," Peter said, **AGREEING WITH ME** when I'd just told him to be his annoying little brother self. I glared at him again. He gave me a nod to say he had this.

"Is Dad off his call yet? This is so boring," Peter said, in his very familiar pest voice. "Baseball's the worst. I guess that makes sense, since you're the worst." Annoying Peter was back, even if it was pretend.

Diego looked over his shoulder at us. "Oh, whew, he is okay." He continued snapping and I breathed a sigh of relief.

As I did, I noticed Coach Daniels across the field and waved. He started to wave until he saw my arm in a cast. Then his face stretched into a scream, like that painting that's actually called *The Scream*. He ran over and said, "What happened? Are you okay?" in a way that made it sound like I'd just cracked my arm right then, in front of him.

"Seattle happened," I said, gloomily. "But it's okay—it's my left arm."

"Wow, stay away from Seattle," Coach said.

"Tell me about it," I said. Coaches could decide where to put you on the field. It was too bad they couldn't decide to keep you in.

But then Diego said, "She might move there!" Oh, ugh. Coach Daniels's face went from relieved to woeful. The number of expressions he had was actually impressive.

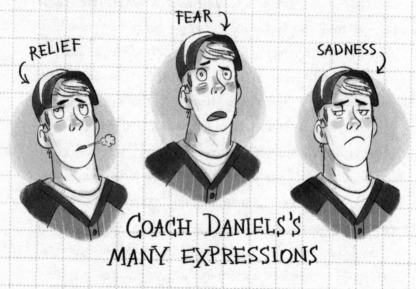

RELIEF

FEAR

SADNESS

COACH DANIELS'S
MANY EXPRESSIONS

"What will Peach Tree be without Gabby Garcia?" he said. Exactly, I thought.

And **THAT** was what I'd meant by "lightning doesn't strike twice." It had been one thing to make it work when

I suddenly had to switch schools and restart my whole life at Piper Bell. I couldn't start fresh again in Seattle. Fresh starts had an expiration date.

I looked at Peter and could tell that he was getting mopey, like me. The walk hadn't helped any new thoughts emerge. But then, Diego sprung a surprise on us. "Oh, I meant to tell you: I saw this contest for the Peach Tree Citizen of the Year and I thought maybe you should enter your dad. Because he's so involved and everything." He shrugged. "If he got it, it would be a cool award to remind him of Peach Tree. When . . . I mean, if, you move. The application is due soon. I just found out about it."

I looked at Peter, who was already looking at me, and I could tell we were thinking the same thing: If you won an award declaring you your town's **TOP CITIZEN**, how could you **EVER LEAVE** that town? Or at least, how could you decide to leave right after getting the award? You couldn't.

At the same time, Peter and I said to Diego: "Where does he sign up?"

Seattle: 4
Peach Tree: 1, but with a BIG IDEA
coming up to bat!

A VIEW TO A PLAY: ENTERING DAD FOR THE COMMUNITY ALLIANCE CITIZEN OF THE YEAR AWARD

So here I am, Playbook, with a new component of the All-Pros Play in motion. Peter and I just downloaded the application. It wasn't hard to fill it out.

Dad did a lot of things in Peach Tree. He was . . .

- Volunteer pancake maker at the Kid Kamp Fund-raising Breakfast every year, and had become the Pancake Grand Poobah

- Host of the monthly Culinary Adventurers Club at the Peach Tree Public Library

- Coach of the Slamming Seniors Softball League

- Founder and head of the "Write On" Bilingual Student Writing Workshop

- Three-time winner of the Peach Tree Chili Cookoff

- Coach or assistant coach of multiple Peach Tree youth baseball and soccer teams

- Winner, MVP, of Peach Tree Parks Department Adult Basketball League

- Author of *Peach Tree: An Appreciative History*, published 2013

"Wow, Dad does a lot of stuff," Peter said.

"I know." I looked over the list. "And you know what? I feel like we're forgetting something."

"Well, I don't think he's ever missed one of my games," Peter said.

"Weird, I don't think he's ever missed one of mine, either," I said.

Peter frowned. "He must have missed one sometime, right? Like if we had games at the same time."

"Maybe he can duplicate himself," I said. "That would be cool if he could share that power. Then maybe a duplicate me and a duplicate you can go live in Seattle."

Peter shook his head. "Let's stop with the sci-fi stuff. We need to write the personal statement," he said. "I'll type, 'cause your arm will slow us down."

PEACH TREE ⚡ SEATTLE
GABBY VS GABBY

I didn't argue because Diego hadn't been kidding about the due date: we had to get the application mailed by tomorrow.

Here's a copy of what we came up with:

> We're submitting our father, Juan Garcia, as a candidate for the Peach Tree Citizen of the Year Award. When we wrote the list of all the things our dad does as a Peach Tree citizen, we were pretty amazed. Actually, we even thought we could just stop filling out all these forms ourselves because it seems like our dad is someone who should be nominated by everyone in town.

But just in case he's not, here's what we can tell you: Juan Garcia isn't just a great person to the town of Peach Tree. He's a great, **GREAT** father to us. How many other people can say that they come up with an easy step-by-step gnocchi tutorial for the Culinary Adventurers who attend his monthly library demonstrations **AND** always make sure their family's favorite taco toppings are available every Taco Tuesday? Or how many people can help students perfect their college essays while also giving insightful notes on their daughter's English Composition papers?

My brother are I are athletes (he plays soccer, I play baseball) and there's a way to describe our dad: best all-around. Sure, there are players who might be better at their specialty, but when you find a player who can do a little bit of everything and do it all well, you're very lucky to have him on your team. Or, to have him live in your town.

By sharing so much of what he loves and who he is, our father Juan Garcia has made Peach Tree a better place to live for so many people, but most of all, he's made it a great place to live for us.

Even if you don't select him, we're grateful we got the chance to see he's not just awesome in person, but he's pretty darn awesome on paper, too.

"If they don't pick Dad after that, I'm going to learn how to make medals so I can give him one," Peter said.

"Nah. We'll make him a trophy. A **BIG** one," I said.

There was a little tiny tear in my eye as I thought about leaving Peach Tree, but also about what would happen to Peach Tree if it lost Dad. Like that old movie *It's A Wonderful Life*, where the town is completely depressing because George Bailey is never born. "Maybe a trophy so big we can't fit it in a box to go to Seattle."

I needed to make the joke so that I wouldn't cry. Dad has always said it's fine to cry but it's also great to laugh when you do.

We printed everything out and walked to the mailbox.

When we dropped it in, I looked at Peter and said, "We need to high-five."

"Isn't this more like a fingers-crossed kind of thing?"

I shook my head.

"No, it's definitely a time for a serious high five. Like one that's really important," I said. "You stand there and I'll face you. We have to take three zen breaths in and out and then high-five slowly, so we barely make a sound. Only the universe can hear it."

Peter gave me a really skeptical look. "This doesn't sound like a thing people do."

"It's what we do. This has to work." I didn't need him questioning my moves right now, so I held up my hand.

"Okay," Peter said. He held up his right hand in high-five position.

"Three zen breaths," I said. "Visualize our victory."

"How do I do that?"

"I guess close your eyes and imagine still living here when you're twelve or something."

"Ah, okay."

We closed our eyes and the picture in my mind was me, taller and a teenager, with my equipment bag and a uniform for Peach Tree High School, walking into the dugout at the high school field. I waved to my parents in the stands, and even to an older version of Peter, who looked much more supportive than I'd ever seen him look at one of my games.

FUTURE PETER

FUTURE GABBY

Welcome to PEACH TREE Home, Sweet Home

"What," I said, opening my eyes. I sort of wanted to see where that visualization had been going.

"Stop your breathing. We need to high-five!"

The Serious High Five only took us a few seconds, but I knew it was the most important high five of my entire life.

So now it's time for bed, Playbook, and I know you're technically just a notebook that I've made a key to my life but in case your powers are as strong as I think, can I just ask that you put all your energy toward keeping me in Peach Tree?

THIS IS NO ORDINARY HIGH FIVE!

THIS HAS TO WORK

I don't want an A for effort,
I don't want a "Nice try, kid!"
'Cause this new plan has to work
Or what's the point of all we did?
This is the big game, **THE SHOW**,
This is the one that counts
If bringing our best doesn't work
Then we've no other plans to mount.
I'm sure Seattle is fine for someone
Its sights to others bring joy
But Peach Tree is my place in the world
Staying here's the cause for this ploy.
To lose this place, my home, my friends,
It's not a loss I can just shirk.
So universe, I'm begging you . . .
This has to, it has to, it has to . . .
Pretty please, it for sure has to work.

GIVE ME A SIGN

 Goal: Get the universe to cooperate
Action: Wish really hard for magic to happen

Post-Day Analysis:
September 23

When people talk about pitchers, they talk about our "stuff." It's a very unspecific way of talking about a very specific thing. A pitcher's "stuff" is all the throws he or she is able to do. Some pitchers aren't that crafty with their pitches but can just throw consistently fast. Some pitchers have a pitch that **ONLY THEY** can throw. Devon is working on a knuckleball that is so slow and unpredictable that a batter might get tired of waiting for it to get to the plate (and swing too early). My slider—which I've already decided to name the Gabby Gotcha—is one that looks like you can hit it dead-on but "escapes" the strike zone just as the batter swings.

I was happy with the application Peter and I had sent in for Dad to win the Peach Tree Citizen of the Year Award, but I was worried it didn't have that zing of being really good **STUFF**. It was strong, but it wasn't **INGENIOUS**.

Piper Bell was moving on in the tournament, and I was sick and tired of being in the dugout. I was jealous that all I had to do was make a deeper butt print in the bench.

As the team clattered into its mitts and tied cleats and chattered around me, I clenched my teeth and tried to think of something big—the Gabby Gotcha plan to stay in Peach Tree—that would save the day.

"Are you okay?" Nolan asked as he sat on the bench next to me. Devon was pitching.

"Not really," I said. "I'm worried I'm going to move." I'd been trying this whole time not to tell anyone that I was afraid the move would really happen, but knowing Nolan had his own family things to deal with made it easier to be honest with him. Plus, sometimes it was easier to tell someone you barely knew the things that bothered you.

"Have you thought about telling your parents you hate the idea?"

"Sure, but it's kind of like you and baseball," I said. "I want to **SHOW** them we should stay here, not tell them."

Nolan nodded. "Now that my parents are watching these games, they've started to understand why I like playing baseball so much," he said. "They still wish I loved tennis, but they like that I'm happy."

On the field, Devon had a batter on first taking a big leadoff, and she snapped around to make the throw before the runner could see her. She got him out as he tried to get back to his base.

"No one should ever steal anything from Devon," Nolan said.

"I know, right?"

It was nice, for once, to watch a game with a friend. I relaxed and leaned back with my head against the dugout wall. For about two seconds.

Until Madeleine huffed in and tossed her backpack under the bench. Madeleine has never quite liked me, because the first time we met was by me smashing into her in the outfield and giving her a bloody nose.

"I need to talk to Gabby," she announced in a gruff voice, sending the team members who weren't on the field scattering. Then she plopped on the bench next to me. "I need your advice."

"What?" I almost jumped.

"Yeah, you helped Nolan and Mario and maybe you can help me."

I wondered if this were a trick. But then Madeleine started talking.

"The problem is, I'm trying to do everything and it's not fair," she said.

"Uhhh . . . ." My brain was trying to make me sound insightful but my mouth was stuck. "Can you . . . do less?"

"No!" she said, like I'd asked the world's worst question. "I need good grades but I want to play baseball and I take all the hardest classes but those take away from me ever getting to be as good as someone who can work at their sport."

This still felt like at trick. "And you can't be in two places at once."

"No!" Everything Madeleine said sounded urgent. "It shouldn't have to be so hard!" I'd known what to say to Mario and Nolan, but Madeleine didn't have the yips. She was plain angry. I sort of understood because under all the planning and scheming and playmaking, I was a little angry, too. I didn't want to have to do so much work to keep my life the same. I also didn't know what to tell Madeleine. I looked around to see if one of our teammates could help, but everyone had moved to the other end of the dugout.

"I wish everyone knew what it was like to have the same pressures as me, on the field and off, but that's just not possible . . ."

"Maybe you just want someone to tell you you're doing a good job?" I smiled at her. "You're doing a good job." I patted her shoulder, wondering if this was the start of a great friendship.

Madeleine rolled her eyes. Nope. "It would be nicer to level the playing field and have everyone have to deal with all the stuff I have to. There's a science fair project due the same day as the last tournament game!"

What had she said?

Level the playing field.

Level. The. Playing. Field.

Level the playing field!

That was it. If I couldn't make Peach Tree beat out Seattle with its own merits, couldn't I just make Peach Tree have the **SAME THINGS** Seattle was offering?

"You're a genius," I told Madeleine. The universe must have heard me wishing for a great idea and sent an answer in the form of someone who didn't really like me!

"At least someone thinks so," she muttered.

I couldn't stay for the rest of the game. I had a plan and I had to act on it immediately.

When you've got the stuff, you've gotta use it.

If Dad could have the same job in Peach Tree (or at least close by, like Atlanta) as he would in Seattle, there was no way we'd move.

THIS was it.

I jumped up and hugged Madeleine. It was very awkward because of my cast, and because she definitely did not want to be hugged.

"Just pay more attention when you're on the field," I told Madeleine. "You're always thinking about the other things you have to do and it's not helping." It was rushed but honest. You had to be in the game to have a good game.

ME + MADELEINE = AWKWARD HUG CENTRAL

Then I told Coach Hollylighter I had to leave. "But if this works, I'll be starting next season!" I booked it out of the dugout to go home. The **HOME** I was never leaving.

Judy: *Bob, I have to say I'm proud*

of Gabby. For the last few weeks, her plans to stay in Peach Tree have been minor league. And now with this idea . . .

Bob: *She's playing in a major league kind of way!*

Judy: *Righto. The question is, does she have enough time to make this work?*

Bob: *Gabby is always up for a ninth-inning save.*

Peach Tree: 1
Seattle: 4...

But everything is about to change . . . right?

THE LEVEL
THE PLAYING FIELD

Goal: Make staying in Peach Tree as enticing if not better than moving to Seattle

Action: Show Atlanta papers what they're missing, and get them to hire one Juan Garcia

Post-Day Analysis:
September 24

At first, Peter was a little nervous about my idea. "We're going to apply for a job for Dad at the *Atlanta Herald*?" He made a strange face, like this:

EYEBROW DOING SOMETHING TWITCHY

MOUTH UNSURE WHETHER TO SMILE ☺ OR FROWN ☹

NOSTRILS ALL PINCHY LOOKING

PETER'S <u>EXTREMELY</u> SKEPTICAL FACE

"Yes, it's perfect."

"We're thirteen and nine. That adds up to twenty-two. That's barely old enough to apply for a job that requires **EXPERIENCE**. Dad's like a million."

I waved him off. "But we have expertise. We **KNOW** Dad. And we have the internet!"

I had my browser open to a page about putting together a writing portfolio and composing a letter to potential employers.

"I don't know," he said. "Shouldn't we just stick to the original plan?"

I told him that—as brilliant as the original plan was—this wasn't about making Peach Tree seem better than Seattle but about evening things out.

"So, this way, Dad gets his dream job here and we get to stay and nobody is disappointed about missing out on **ANYTHING**."

"Ahh," he said. He got it.

And, after years of not getting along, we somehow wrote a letter that made me think the *Atlanta Herald* should hire US for a job.

Dear Ms. Klemson,

I'm a longtime reader of your fine paper, the *Atlanta Herald*, in particular your excellent sports section. The only thing better than reading it, in fact, would be writing for it. As a writer, an editor, and someone who's lived in the area as a devoted sports fan, I feel I can bring something excellent to your pages: my voice, full time. My writing has been featured in your pages a number of times, from columns about the best place to get a coffee and good conversation (Sweeten the Pot is my favorite) to profiles of citizens who contribute in ways that sometimes go unnoticed (the peanut vendor at Braves games who also treats families who've never been to a game to free seats) and myriad other topics of interest to area readers.

The thing is, my work for the *Atlanta Herald* might come to a sad end. I'm in the running for a position at the *Seattle Gazette*, as a full-time sports reporter. It's definitely a win, personally, but I'm hoping to score a win-win for my family. They'd hate to leave our home here, and I feel the same. I've been in this area for more than twenty years, and the connections I've made with the community have been great for my work. Reporting with heart is easier when your heart is in the right place.

I hope you will consider my application, and I hope to hear from you soon. I've included samples from my portfolio as well as a list of books I've contributed to or edited.

Sincerely,

Juan Garcia

(*Myriad* was one of my vocabulary words this week, by the way, meaning "many." But it sounded like the word choice of someone who could have any job he wanted!)

For working in an office with papers and books piled up everywhere (unlike the pantry, Dad didn't seem in a hurry to empty this room out), Dad's files were surprisingly organized on his computer, and we were able to print out a lot of his best work.

We put everything in a big yellow envelope and wrote the address as neatly as we could on the front.

"How will he get a job somewhere that's not advertising the job?" Peter asked.

"I don't know, maybe because if you can get a great player, you don't want to lose them to someone else," I said. "And, Dad always says you'll never know unless you try."

"Yeah, his vocal cords have dents in the shape of those words."

"I think Grandma says it, so maybe it's hereditary."

"Let's get to the mailbox," Peter said. "We need to do another serious high five."

Peach Tree: 1
Seattle: 4 (but about to be thrown out of the game!)

THE KEEP IT
UNDER YOUR HAT

Goal: Don't jinx the plan by talking about it
Action: Contain myself during yet another (unneeded) memory-making session

Post-Day Analysis:
September 25

For the first time since the possible Seattle move had been announced, I felt calm. Good, even. When Diego texted to invite me to yet another memory-making farewell get-together—watching movies at his house, with his mom's excellent cheddar popcorn—I didn't get prickly.

In fact, I was so excited about everything working out that I didn't want to potentially ruin the surprise. That's why people like sports so much: no spoilers. Even the best predictors in the world didn't get every game outcome correct. My and Peter's plan **HAD** to work, and I was confident it would, but it was better not to give any details away.

"Gabby, it's so good to see you," Mrs. Parker said, greeting me at the door. "How have you been doing with . . . everything?" Before she became a florist, Mrs. Parker had studied to be a guidance counselor. Sometimes she still slipped into that mode. It probably explained why Diego was so well-adjusted. She was never pushy about wanting to give advice, but you could always tell when she thought you could use a talk.

ANITA PARKER

DIEGO'S MOM

Height: Makes it clear where Diego gets it from

Build: Narrow but strong

Sport: Competitive flower arranging

Excels at: Making bouquets, sniffing out kids who need to talk

Favorite Athlete: Whoever is getting her fantasy baseball team the most points that season

Motto: "The power of finding beauty in the humblest things makes home happy and life lovely."—Louisa May Alcott

I panicked for a second. I was actually **GREAT**! But what kid who potentially was moving away from her school and friends was great?

Bob: *Gabby needs to be very careful with this.*

Judy: *You're right, Bob! If she plays it too sad, Mrs. Parker might get so concerned she tells Gabby's parents—who don't know quite how upset she was about the move.*

Bob: *But if she gives any kind of tip-off that she's not worried about moving because she has the situation under control, that's also a red flag.*

"I'm, um, trying to make the best of everything," I said. This was 100 percent true!

It worked. "Oh, honey." Ms. Parker put her arm around my good arm and squeezed lightly. "It will all work out for the best."

"I hope so," I said, thinking of the job application we'd sent, and how happy Dad would be if it actually worked.

"The kids are in the TV room," she said. "They'll be so glad to see you."

Johnny, Diego, and Katy were already there . . . sitting on pillows around the Parkers' coffee table . . .

Or I thought they were . . . it was so loaded with snacks
I could barely see my friends' faces!

It was a buffet of treats: the cheddar popcorn but also a
zoo's worth of gummies (not just bears, but also worms,
monkeys, and sharks!), Milk Duds, red licorice, and even
my favorite hate-to-
love-them candy, Sour
Patch Kids.

They also had made
a sign with the movie
choices for the night.

"What is this?" I
asked.

"We couldn't find
any other movies about
Seattle precisely, but

MOVIE NIGHT:

1. THE SANDLOT
2. THE NATURAL
3. FIELD OF DREAMS
4. SLEEPLESS IN SEATTLE

* 2 AND 3 ARE 📽))
BASEBALL MOVIES
THAT ARE GOOD
BUT ALSO
VERY MUCH FOR DADS.

we thought we could watch that one and make fun of Seattle," Johnny said. "To cheer you up."

"We know you're gonna be awesome there," Katy said. "But we still don't think that city deserves you."

"Or, we could just watch *The Sandlot* if you'd rather do that," Diego said. "We should have let you pick the movies."

"No, this is great," I said, even though a week ago I might not have felt this way. The fact that Peter and I had two good Stay in Peach Tree plays in motion made my friends' sympathy easier to take. "Thanks, guys. Let's watch the Seattle one."

Diego clicked on the remote but Katy stopped him. "Before we start, should we do our Gabby Lists?"

Diego slapped his forehead. "Oh, yeah! Gabby Lists."

"What are you guys talking about?" I asked.

Katy was already standing in front of the TV and had pulled a set of index cards from her pocket.

"We made lists," she said. "Or, like, notes, about you. And what we will miss about you. **IF** you go."

She'd called it an **IF**! "It's a big **IF**," I said, bursting to tell them about what I'd done. But Katy was already clearing her throat.

"I'm going to miss the way Gabby is always ready for anything, and how she gets as excited as I do about a new

225

song or a challenge. A lot of people know how to come through for you when you're down, but I sometimes think not as many know how to be up for you when you're winning," Katy read. "I haven't had a partner like that ever." She looked like she was going to cry. Then I almost started to cry.

"I'm not gone yet," I said, wiping my eyes. *Or at all,* I thought.

"I know," Katy said, as I stood up and gave her a hug. "You're the best, GG."

"You, too, KH."

I once saw a TV show where an old man fakes his death so he can go to his own funeral to hear if people would say nice things about him. This was exactly like that and I didn't even have to pretend to be dead!

Johnny's turn was next. He wasn't a performer like Katy, and he looked kind of nervous getting up there. (He'd looked the same way practicing his speech for class president, but it was a great speech.) He straightened his tie and read from his clipboard. "I'm going to miss how Gabby always has a plan. She's like math."

"Wait, what?" Diego said. "Math??"

"That came out weird, but let me finish . . ." I smiled up at Johnny and he straightened his already-straight tie again.

"In math, there's one right answer, but you can think about a problem in a bunch of ways. Gabby does that, and she never seems worried about not finding the answer. She's just full of different solutions. But I also like how she's the opposite of math because she dives in to things that might not even have an answer. And, I like her red high-tops and how whenever I see her, it makes me smile." He rushed that last part.

Then Johnny turned as red as my high-tops and I did, too. I quickly gulped a Sour Patch Kid so that my face would do something besides blush.

MY
SOUR CANDY
≡LOVE-HATE≡
RELATIONSHIP...

Diego stood up and didn't read from anything.
"I'm not going to miss Gabby," he started.

WHAT? I thought.

"What?" Katy said.

"You can't miss someone who's like a part of you. I figured that out when I was in Costa Rica. We're best friends for life and so I can't really get rid of her, even if I tried."

Everyone laughed. Even me.

"But I will miss things about her. She's funny and she's not afraid to fall down or get things wrong. Even if when she does get things wrong, she usually thinks she's right for a while before she admits it," he said. That part was a little true. "She helped me learn to ride a bike by just being so good at it she made it look easy. I'm not looking forward to her being all the way in Seattle, that's for sure. But I can't ever think of her as **GONE**."

He came and hugged me and then Katy and Johnny joined in and by the time we started *Sleepless in Seattle*, I was teary-eyed, even if Johnny was holding my hand on the couch. I missed the first part of the movie while I tried to memorize everything everyone had said so that I could write it down now, at home. (You can't really be sneaky with a playbook when your friends are watching your every move.)

During *Sleepless in Seattle*—which didn't make Seattle look as totally awful as it is and was kind of a sweet

228

movie even if it was also about grown-ups falling in love a million years ago by hearing each other on the radio and really what kind of problems did they have if they never had to text each other?—my friends worked extra hard to point out what was wrong with the city. I sat in the dark, kind of grinning stupidly.

THINGS MY FRIENDS SAID ABOUT SEATTLE DURING SLEEPLESS IN SEATTLE

- Why would anyone make a landmark look like a needle? Was a tower too awesome? —Johnny

- If I were there, I'd sleep all the time. It looks like a snooze. —Katy

- Of course they have to meet at the Empire State Building. You can't be romantic in a Space Needle. —Diego

- Well, maybe the people will be nice? —Katy

- You'll probably make a ton of new friends right away. —Johnny

- You do love a good rainstorm. —Diego

There were two reasons for my grin:

229

My friends really cared about me. A lot.

I was going to be able to make them all incredibly happy when I told them that I'd fixed everything!

After hearing what my friends said—that I was a can-do person who always had a plan—I was so tempted to reveal the Stay in Peach Tree plays—especially the job application we'd sent for Dad—so they'd see I wasn't letting them down. But I had to keep it quiet.

It was better to surprise them, even if they seemed to know I could do it all along.

Peach Tree: 1 (but with plays in motion) Seattle: 4

(But really, how could Seattle possibly win when it is so clear that **THIS** is where I need to be??)

THE FORFEIT

Forfeiting is when you realize you need to stop playing. It's usually not for reasons you're going to love.

"Gabby, I need to talk to you" is how this play starts.

It also starts with my skin getting cold and a weird sweat coating appearing on top of it. Sweating when you're cold is a horrible sensation.

I knew by the way my dad said my name that he had **NEWS**.

But was it good news or bad news?

"Okay, Dad," I said brightly, trying to steer the news to the good side.

"Let's go outside." He opened the patio door and brought

his coffee cup with him. It was a mug I'd gotten him that had a smiley face on it and said "My Mug Looks Better When It's Filled With Coffee." (Get it?)

He sat down and took a sip of coffee and looked out over the backyard. "It's really nice out, isn't it?" he said, exactly like a person in a coffee commercial. "The leaves are finally starting to turn, too. Look at your tree."

My tree was a sugar maple at the far edge of our back-yard. When I was little I called it my tree because its trunk was curved in just enough that it fit me perfectly, like a hug. We had a pretty magnolia tree in our front yard but the maple in the back was my favorite.

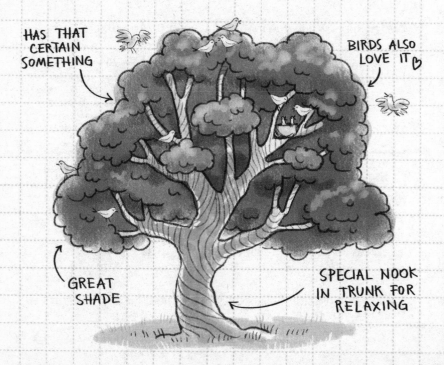

HAS THAT CERTAIN SOMETHING

BIRDS ALSO LOVE IT

GREAT SHADE

SPECIAL NOOK IN TRUNK FOR RELAXING

We both looked at it for a few seconds in a calm, peaceful way. I relaxed. I thought, the way this was all going, we had to be staying in Peach Tree. Maybe the Citizen of the Year Award and the job application didn't even need to work, because I felt like Dad was about to say he'd decided he liked things the way they were. If it was a "we're moving" chat, would he really be talking about the tree and the leaves, and sipping his coffee so slowly, like someone so happy to be **RIGHT WHERE HE WAS**?

But even though I felt sure things were going to go my way, the waiting was driving me nuts!

"So . . . what did you want to talk about?" I asked.

"Well . . . ," Dad started. He took another sip of his coffee. **WHAT WAS HE DOING? THIS WAS TORTURE! THE LEAVES ON MY TREE WERE GOING TO ALL TURN COLOR AND FALL OFF IF HE DIDN'T SAY SOMETHING SOON!** He cleared his throat and looked at me, then said, in the same very even tone: "I need to know what on earth you were thinking when you sent a job application to the *Atlanta Herald* in my name."

Was he happy about whatever on earth I'd been thinking . . . or not so happy? Usually with my dad, I can tell in an instant how he's feeling. So can everyone. His eyes flash in a certain way when he's glad and his mouth gets really stitched together when he's upset. But today, his eyebrows were just raised. I didn't know what that expression meant, except that he was curious.

So I asked, "Did you get the job?"

"No. There's no job there," he said. And **NOW** he pressed his lips together. He was **NOT HAPPY**. His mouth was angry and his eyes were sad.

My stomach plunged down so fast it felt like my whole body was going to flatten itself.

Then it got worse. My dad used **THE TONE**. He almost never uses **THE TONE**, but when he does, it means things really went wrong and he's displeased. The last time I heard him use it was when our fridge broke out of nowhere and he called the warranty line and they told him the warranty was no longer valid even though it was. The tone isn't mean, so much as factual, but the facts he gives are never in the other person's favor.

Here were the facts he gave me: "There's a job in Seattle. A job I was offered. A job the managing editor called me about today to ask if I really wasn't interested in relocation. A friend of hers in Atlanta had *also* gotten an application, making it seem I'd rather be in Georgia. And guess what I said to that?"

I looked down, wondering if now was a bad time to point out how long he'd had that mug I'd given him and how it sure seemed to be his favorite. "Did you say that you didn't even apply to that job?" I asked softly.

"You bet I did. And then what do you think I did?"

"You wondered who applied to that job for you?"

He nodded. And then he started a speech with my full name: Gabrielle.

Playbook, did you even **KNOW** that's my full name?

NO. Or, maybe you do. But basically, no one calls me that. I've been called that only about eight times since I was born and always at serious moments. Not even **IN-TROUBLE** serious moments, but **SERIOUS** like talking to me about how my mom had died, or when Dad was going to marry Louie, or when I was going to have a baby brother.

But now it was a serious and, I think, in-trouble moment.

Dad started to talk about how hard it is to get great jobs at great newspapers and especially for sportswriters and he was very lucky that he hadn't been counted out of the Seattle job instantly based on someone assuming that his heart wasn't in it and . . . as he told me all of this, I realized something.

I had made a play that had hurt my teammate.

My numero uno teammate: my dad.

It was worse than committing an error in a game, because an error, even if it screws up the score, isn't something you **TRIED TO DO**. And this whole time, I'd been **TRYING** at the All-Pros Play. I'd **WANTED** to jinx the job.

"I'm sorry," I said to him, when he finally finished. And I really was. But saying sorry felt about as useful as a broken refrigerator.

"I know," Dad said. "And when they called me, I started to figure it out: you'd told Grandma my news, you took me to Casa de Mayo and spilled the beans, you and Peter . . . are you working together to try to keep us here?"

I looked at the ground, then at my tree. "We are," I said, but added, "But this was all me. Or all my idea. I just wanted to bring what you wanted in Seattle to Peach Tree."

Dad put his hands in the air, like whatever could make staying here possible was way out of his reach.

"I've been freelance writing for years, Gabby," he said. "And the dream was always that someday, when you kids were older, I could go back to work full-time, if I could find the right job, and if it was really worth it. We've always been a team, and then I find out that not only don't you want to go, but you almost sabotaged the dream?"

He was right, of course. The All-Pros Play wasn't as much about Dad as it was about me. And Peter. But honestly, mostly me. Peter had signed up to help me, but I was the one who'd started all this.

I was still staring at my tree as my eyes filled with tears. It had been there when it was just me and Dad. It had seen me and Dad when we were our saddest together and later when we were happier, playing catch in the yard. It had been there when I first got hit with a baseball in the exact arm that was now in the cast and I cried a little. I'd cried not because it hurt but because I didn't understand why Dad had thrown it like that and Dad had almost cried because he'd made a bad throw, and he'd hugged me and when he said sorry he reminded me he was always on my team and would never do anything to hurt me, his numero uno teammate.

But the Seattle idea **HAD** hurt me. As I wiped my eyes, I felt a little like he was to blame, too.

"I just wish you had asked me what I thought," I said. "This isn't like your plans that never really happen, like how you daydream about opening a restaurant, or writing a novel. At first, it felt like something I could change, and then it kept feeling more real but like no one cared what I thought, or at least wanted to make sure I was okay about it. I still wouldn't like it, but it wouldn't seem so unfair."

"I'm sorry, too," he said. "I forget sometimes because you're so much like me that you're not actually sharing my brain and I have to tell you things more clearly. This happened quickly, and I didn't think about how to communicate it."

"So does that mean we're definitely moving?"

"I have a lot of smoothing over to do, with the *Atlanta Herald* and the *Seattle Gazette*," he said. "I think I can work it out and tell them my kids are a little emotional right now. I'm the front-runner but I think the hiring committee might have some doubts. They need to hear from me that I really am serious about the job."

Was he saying that he was going to get the job in Seattle but might not now? Because of what we'd—what I'd—done? It was what I'd wanted: for Seattle not to work out. But not because my dad lost his shot at a dream job. And not because I'd ruined it for him. The point of the All-Pros Play had been to make Dad and Louie decide they wanted to stay here, **NOT** to take away the option of leaving. Even though he didn't seem like he was going to punish me, it was worse to see my dad so sad because of me.

It was even worse than the other thing: that the play was over, and I might have to face the facts that Seattle wasn't going away, and the Garcias were probably going. My dad was the front-runner, and he really wanted the job.

The only way Seattle wouldn't happen was if I'd truly messed everything up. But there was no way I could call the play a success if it meant that I'd abandoned my team to make it work.

Seattle: 4
Peach Tree: 1
Final

THE ALL-PROS PLAN: A WRAP-UP

When I told Peter what had happened, he didn't make fun of me, or tease me, or say my idea had been stupid and I sure proved I was the silly big sister he'd always thought I was.

It was way worse.

He just looked . . . . disappointed.

"Oh, well, I guess that's it, then," he said. And he shrugged.

His disappointment, I should add, seemed like it was **IN ME**.

If he'd said something like, "Oh, well, what could we expect from someone who trips over hot dogs?" it would have been better.

Because at least then things would have felt the same as before we started working together.

Instead, it was like I lost *two* Peters—the annoying one and the new one, who was kind of a good brother. Probably even a great brother. And if I was going to lose my hometown, too, I really needed my brother.

BEST NIGHT EVER
(YEAH, RIGHT)

Goal: Have a good time when I officially feel like a loser
Action: Worry about my friends having a good time, instead of wallowing in my misery

Post-Play Analysis:
September 29

The only thing worse than feeling sorry for yourself might be feeling like other people are feeling sorry for you.

Now that my All-Pros Play has failed, I have to face facts: my friends totally feel sorry for me, and it's totally warranted.

And I know what they feel like. Sometimes experiencing someone else's crushing defeat hits you way harder than handling your own.

That sounds **BONKERS**, I know. And, okay, Playbook, when I started you, all my focus was on keeping my wins going, but I figured this one thing out: when you're losing, you're still kind of in control. Even when my win streak felt like it was slipping away back in the spring, or this summer when I thought Diego was bailing on our friendship, I could make new moves and try new strategies.

When you're still playing, losing doesn't totally exist because you could be on your way to a win.

Even when you do lose, you can at least wonder how you will fix it next time.

But when *someone else* is losing, you feel hopeless.

When a major league game is on TV, and a pitcher I love is on the mound and everything's going wrong, and they have too many runners on base and things are crumbling, I get this awful feeling in my stomach for them, because I can't do anything to fix it. I can only watch and hope and clench my teeth and cross my fingers and feel all sick for them. But I can't get on the mound. (Though what a cool thing that might be, to just zap myself into a major league game.)

I worry about that pitcher long after the coach has put in a reliever and even after the game's over, because I know that—even if they're used to it on some level—pitchers beat themselves up when they have a bad game.

So, to my friends, my tragic probably-move to Seattle must feel like the saddest thing on earth. They're working so hard to make me feel good but I know it's because they think my life is going down the toilet.

And, the way I feel today, I don't totally disagree with them.

Which leads me to: the Parks Department Mixer. Mixer as in a dance where you mix with other kids from the community.

My friends want to go, and bring me, and make memories, and generally believe that their efforts are pulling me out of the toilet. Which is noble, because who wants to touch a toilet-water person?

But I don't really want to go. Why mix if I'll just have to **UNMIX** if and when we move?

They're insistent, though.

Katy just sent me a topple of texts (my word for a group of texts from the same person):

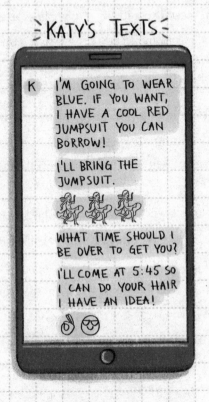

KATY'S TEXTS

K I'M GOING TO WEAR BLUE. IF YOU WANT, I HAVE A COOL RED JUMPSUIT YOU CAN BORROW!

I'LL BRING THE JUMPSUIT.

WHAT TIME SHOULD I BE OVER TO GET YOU?

I'LL COME AT 5:45 SO I CAN DO YOUR HAIR I HAVE AN IDEA!

I should go. Why make my friends feel worse for me, right?

(Pause for mixer preparation and attendance)

When Katy showed up with a curling iron, I plastered on a smile and sat on my bed while she curled and sprayed and chatted.

"So, do you think I should do 'Seize the Day' and 'Flip Your Lid'?" she was asking. Katy had been asked to sing two songs at the mixer during DJ breaks. "I mean, it's not really a big deal, oh, never mind." She was trying to down-play being excited about the performance. You know, like people do when their life is going great and yours is toilet-y. But I was excited for her, even if I wasn't excited for me.

"Definitely those two," I said, wondering who Katy would replace me with if I left. She probably had people applying to be her new friend and occasional song-writing partner. "My hair's already curly . . . What are you doing to it?"

She cocked her head to one side: "Giving you a **LOOK**." She turned my shoulders so I could see the mirror and, well, I looked like someone who had her life under control. Because my hair looked awesome: she'd straightened the top and swooped the whole jumble to one side and then created a bunch of curls bursting over my left shoulder.

"Oh my gosh," I said.

"You look amazing," she said and then handed me a bag. "Here." Her jumpsuit looked **SUPER COOL** when I put it on. "Put on your red high-tops, of course," Katy instructed.

Katy was wearing a blue jumpsuit with rainbow patches on each shoulder. Standing next to each other, we looked like co-stars on a TV show. Except, inside, I still wasn't looking forward to the night ahead.

247

But, writing this now, maybe I should have looked forward to it. Because the mixer was **GREAT**.

The Joyce Winston Rec Center gym had been decorated with streamers and a balloon archway when you walked in, and disco lights shone everywhere. Normally, walking into a place so fancy would have made me wonder what to do, but with Katy next to me, I was only mildly uncomfortable.

Mostly, I was sort of excited, even though I'd planned not to be. Kids from all the middle schools in the area were there, and everyone was clustered in small groups. Everyone was looking at the dance floor but no one was on it, **DANCING**. It felt like people **WANTED** to, though, and the whole gym pulsed with anticipation. (The fact that **EVERYONE** seemed mildly uncomfortable made me feel slightly more comfortable.)

Diego and Johnny were coming together, but I didn't see them yet, and with the flashing lights, I couldn't quite make out people as they entered from the other side of the room. "I can't believe no one's dancing," Katy said.

"Someone will, maybe Diego," I told her. "Or you could."

Katy shook her head. "It's one thing to perform in front of hundreds of people and a totally different thing to walk out in the middle of a mixer and dance alone." If Katy wasn't brave enough to start the dancing, who was?

I looked toward the door for Johnny and Diego. "I think I see them."

I went out into the middle of the empty gym and shielded my eyes with my cast arm. I saw Diego and Johnny standing in the doorway, peering around for me and Katy. I waved my other arm in the air. I didn't realize that with my bent cast arm over my eyes and my other arm extended in a wave, I appeared to be doing an outdated dance move.

AM I "DABBING" ???

"She's dabbing!" someone screamed.

"Do people still dab?" someone else said.

"I guess so!"

"Whatever it takes to get the party started!"

"Looks like we have our first dancer on the floor," the DJ said in a deep voice that filled the room. Then, everything got brighter. There was a spotlight on me.

I was frozen there in my dabbing pose until the DJ said, "Who else has courage enough to get out there?" So I gave my legs a slight bend. I definitely wasn't cut out to be a solo dancer, but why kill the mood? People started to come onto the dance floor and it was all because of me. And my broken-armed, accidental dance moves.

Johnny and Diego made their way to me as the floor filled up.

Johnny was wearing a red tie that matched my vest. "Katy told me what to wear," he said shyly. Playbook, I haven't mentioned it, but Johnny lost the election to Cassie Jacobs. I guess good hair like hers really mattered to voters. The really great thing about Johnny was he bounced back from his loss quickly, and Cassie was smart enough to ask him to be her policy adviser.

"Me, too," I said. "She did a good job."

Katy ran up. "GG! Look at all the people you got on the floor!" She gestured to the crowds of kids now dancing around us. "Amazing!"

She grinned at Johnny. "Told you the tie worked," she said, and then smiled at Diego. "You look nice."

She was right. My best friend had on a **SUIT** and, as he showed us all, **BIRD SOCKS**.

Then my three bestest friends and I formed a loose circle as more of our friends sauntered up to join us. Everyone was dressed up. Even Mario, who I'd never seen wear anything but a baseball uniform or a warm-up suit, had on a shiny jacket and a shirt with buttons.

Devon was wearing one of her Renaissance faire outfits: tall boots, a cape and tunic, and a hat with a giant feather coming out the top. "My mom wanted me to wear a dress, but this is more me," she told us. As usual, you couldn't argue with Devon.

We danced for a long time to the upbeat music the DJ was playing until it was time for Katy to go on. Everyone in the place turned to the stage to watch as she did "Flip Your Lid," and—because it was her song with a million views on YouTube—the whole crowd knew the dance moves. I was trying to keep up but my cast kept bumping Diego so I stopped for a minute.

Then, I saw Madeleine over at the edge of the dance floor. I still felt bad for running out on her the other day, so I excused myself to talk to her.

"Hey, why don't you get on the floor?" I said.

She had her arms folded over her chest and looked stressed. "Nah, I'm not much of a dancer," she said.

"Neither am I," I said. "Neither is Mario. Or Devon."

I pointed out our teammates. Mario was shifting from foot to foot uncomfortably. Devon looked noble in her fancy Renaissance gear but the most she would do was bob her head every so often.

Madeleine . . . blushed. Did she like Mario? Or Devon?

"Come on, it wouldn't hurt you to take a break and go with the flow," I told her. "You work really hard."

Madeleine sighed. "I know, and I should be at home finishing my English essay."

I gently took her by the wrist and pulled her to the dance floor. "Hey!" she said. "What are you doing?"

"Making sure you don't leave."

When Devon and Mario inched over to give her room in their non-dancing semicircle, Madeleine seemed surprised. "I don't know what I'm doing out here," she said.

"No one does," Devon said, and instead of her usual glinty-eyed serious face, she grinned and hopped over a few spaces to make more room for Madeleine to see Katy onstage.

It was the first time in weeks that I really felt like I was part of things. Maybe it was the dancing, or that I was in the action instead of watching it. Or really, maybe it was because I finally had my answer to the move question. I **HATED** the answer, but knowing for sure meant I could finally rest.

So I bobbed along with my friends, trying not to think about Seattle, and after "Seize the Day," Katy wrapped up her act. There was a slight pause and the room buzzed with conversation until the DJ said, "Grab a partner so we can slow things down." The opening of "Top of My World" from the movie *Pizzabird* started to play, and my relief turned to a bubbly fizzing in my stomach. I almost jumped when Johnny tapped my shoulder.

"Do you . . . wanna dance?" he asked, even though we'd been dancing.

"Okay," I said, and wished there was some kind of warm-up for this. Why hadn't I thought to prepare for a **SLOW DANCE?**

It took us a few seconds of watching other slow dancers pair off to figure out where his hands went (my waist) and where mine went (his shoulders). And then you just had to sway, it looked like. This would have been easier if my legs hadn't been so wobbly.

"I hope you guys know, you don't have to feel sorry for me," I said as we finally settled into a swaying rhythm. How could you tell if you were a good slow dancer? Where was a coach when you needed one? I tried to angle my cast arm over his shoulder so it wouldn't be digging into his neck. "I know you and Katy and Diego have been doing all this extra stuff because I'll probably be gone soon." I blurted it out, because it had been on my mind all this time, and he did say he liked that I dived into things.

Johnny shook his head. **VEHEMENTLY.** (That was another new vocabulary word. Meaning "in an intense manner.")

"It's not like that **AT ALL**!" He said it so loud that a few other dancers stopped to look at us.

"But, when I go, you'll all still be here and it will be like I never was here at all," I said, even though admitting it out loud made me feel as nervous as walking onto the mound without my mitt. "You'll forget about me."

I didn't totally believe that, but I believed it a little.

At least I did when it came to Johnny. I knew Diego wouldn't forget me. After all this time, he was sort of stuck with me, like he'd said. And Katy and I would probably still text and get together when she went on tours. But I wasn't as sure about Johnny. He had a big brain, so it was unlikely he'd forget me entirely. But it's not like I had any previous boyfriend experience to base that on.

"You have it all wrong," he said. "We're doing all these memory things because we don't want **YOU** to forget about **US**. Especially me."

My heart started pounding so hard, I almost couldn't hear what Bob and Judy were saying in my brain.

Judy: *For a math whiz, Johnny sure isn't putting together that he equals a* **BIG DEAL** *to Gabby.*

Bob: *If only he knew how much brain space he gets!*

Judy: *Wait, Bob, Johnny looks like he's about to say something important.*

"You're Gabby Garcia," Johnny said. His smile was extra bright under the rainbow lights. "If anyone can go to a whole new town and score points with everyone in it, it's you. Statistically speaking. Because you're amazing."

He looked at me kind of shyly and before I knew what to say, I leaned toward him and kissed him.

For 0.4 seconds.

Right on the lips.

Or, kind of to the right of his lips.

"Um . . . I don't know why I did that." All my little Gabbys were in shock. My face was also in shock.

"I . . . that . . . I'm . . . Please say you're happy you did it?" Johnny said.

I'm pretty sure tiny little hearts were

WHERE MY "KISS" WOUND UP. NOT EXACTLY THE STRIKE ZONE!

bursting out of our heads, like in a cartoon. "I am," I said. "But we should do it again; that was practice. Or, maybe, like we just made the kissing team and I was just figuring out the equipment."

"Yup, you're right, we should definitely do that again," Johnny said, and after what felt like hours of staring at each other that was actually only one verse of the song, we kissed again. For a whole second this time!

HIGHLIGHT REEL: THE KISS

LASTED
ONE
FULL SECOND!

LOOKS LIKE THEY
GOT IT RIGHT!
x x x

ALSO,
FIRST KISS!

THIS IS NICE!
☺

THE LOYAL TEAMMATE

Goal: Honor my commitments
Action: SHOW. UP.

Post-Day Analysis:
September 30

I got my cast off yesterday. My whole family went with me to see Dr. Phillips, who sawed off the cast. She used a small mechanical set of shears that vibrated and whirred like a tiny monster with teeth.

Maybe she did this kind of thing all the time, but to me it was very scary. Also, really smelly. "Oh my gosh, is there an old sock in there?" Peter said, and I stuck my tongue out at him. It was the first normal-ish interaction we'd had since the day Dad had discovered the newspaper plan. I hoped it meant that things between us might stop being so . . . silent.

Dr. Phillips said that since my break was so minimal and the arm had healed so well, I could technically be on the field for the last game of the tournament. "Are you sure, Doc?" Dad said. "I'd love to see her play but . . ."

"She shouldn't bat, or pitch, or be anywhere where she might have to catch a high-velocity ball or really any ball, but if it's important to her, she can symbolically join the game. Somewhere low-action."

"Right field?" I asked.

Dr. Phillips nodded. "As long as you don't do much at all."

That didn't sound exactly like playing to me, but the idea of being on a field made my fingers tingle. Or maybe that was the aftereffect of getting a cast off. Probably that.

Louie and Dad gave me funny looks as we walked to the car. Maybe because I was semi-skipping. "Hmm, someone looks happy," Louie said.

I wondered if they could tell I'd had my first kiss. The thought made me red all over. "I'm glad the cast is off," I said, which was half true. The whole truth was, for a second, I'd forgotten about the Seattle move. The only thing that could stop it at this point was if the application to the *Atlanta Herald* meant the *Seattle Gazette* changed its mind about Dad. If that happened, I was going to blame myself for screwing things up for him, so there was **NO WAY TO WIN**.

"We are, too," Dad said, and squeezed the top of my ponytail. Even though I hadn't gotten punished for the newspaper scheme, things with Dad and me had been sort of like things with Peter and me: kind of quiet. "You've had a rough few weeks, kiddo." When he said that, I felt a little bit better. It seemed like proof he wasn't mad at me, and also like he finally understood that the Seattle thing was a big deal.

I knew that no matter what happened, Dad and Louie and now Peter, too, would be there for me. And it was with that in mind that I showed up at the game. Piper Bell, with only one loss, would be going up against Luther, who also had one loss, to see who would take first place.

I went to wish the team luck in the dugout. I had my bag of gear, and Devon spotted it immediately. "Gabby has her stuff," she said. "She can play?"

"Devon can't pitch at all today, because she's been shoot-ing SECRET arrows and her tendons are sore," Mario said. "Say you'll pitch!"

"You told Coach your secret?"

Devon shrugged. "I have to be me." Then she turned to

me. "So, are you pitching?" she asked, and I caught Nolan watching us.

"Pitching? Didn't she just get her cast off?" Coach Hollylighter looked a little frazzled. I'd never seen her that way. "It would help. Nolan could use a backup. But you can't . . . What did the doctor say?"

"That I can play, if I go easy, or really, if I play symbolically . . ."

"What does that mean?" Devon said. "It's not like you broke your pitching arm."

That was true. And also true was that I felt great. Like I **COULD** play. Could pitch even. Old Gabby might have reassured her team that she could still throw just fine and taken the mound.

But sidelined Gabby . . .

. . . had a rubbery-feeling arm and didn't have any idea what playing **SYMBOLICALLY** even meant. Dr. Phillips wasn't a sports person, clearly.

"I don't know," I said to Coach Hollylighter. "It seems like it's better for everyone if I stay on the sidelines today."

Coach Hollylighter squinted at me. "You sure?"

"Yeah." I nodded. "I can hang here for moral support." I looked around the dugout, hoping someone might need an extra mental boost and I could be dugout therapist again.

I'd really liked helping my teammates. Today, though, everyone was getting their gear on. The team was well-adjusted. And I guess I was, too, more or less.

Nolan was oiling his glove. "You think you're okay to go out there?" I asked him.

He slipped his hand into the mitt and squeezed it in and out three times. A trick I'd taught him. "I can do it."

I stepped out of the dugout when I saw Johnny standing at the fence with his clipboard. "Hi," I said.

"Hi," he said.

We smiled goofily at each other. Would I ever find someone I could be as happy to be awkward with as I was with Johnny?

"You got your cast off," he said.

"I did!" I said.

Then we did the smiling thing again.

I was trying to figure out a way to describe getting my cast off that didn't involve mentioning the bad smell when the game began. Nolan started out strong. When he threw his first pitch, it zoomed past the batter before she even had time to see it.

"Chao looks like he's ready to take home a trophy," I heard someone on the bleachers say.

"He's gotten better since you talked to him," Johnny

said. He held up his clipboard of numbers. "Even statistically speaking."

And he had. Nolan kept the Lions to just a few runs for most of the game. His parents even had made a sign for him that they held up. For people who weren't into baseball, they sure looked like they were enjoying themselves.

Mario came through with a sacrifice fly in the fifth that drove in a run, and Madeleine homered in the sixth.

"I'm going with the flow," she said to me with a very un-Madeleine wink.

But Nolan's arm started to wear down in the seventh. I would have loved to go in but my left arm started tingling, reminding me that this wasn't my game to play.

Devon finally came in to relieve Nolan in the eighth, but she didn't have her stuff. The Lions scored three runs on her, and Piper Bell lost, 6-3. But Piper Bell still got a third-place medal, and the kids clubs got a lot of money for playground equipment.

Devon came back shaking her head. "I need to learn to shoot arrows with the opposite arm," she said. "I really blew that."

"If anyone can figure out how to be an archery expert and a star pitcher, it's you," I told her. "It stinks I won't be here to see it."

"I keep thinking you *have* to be," Devon said. She didn't

blink when she added, "I can't really imagine playing without you."

"Me neither," Nolan said, stepping into our circle. He was holding out his medal to me. "I thought you should have this. For the help you gave me."

I love prizes. Especially shiny ones, like medals and trophies. But I told Nolan no thank you. "You should keep that. It's your first prize as a Penguin," I said. "And since you're going to be one of the starting pitchers this spring, it'll be good to have a lucky charm."

Nolan looked surprised. "Starting? Nah, if you're back, there's no way I'll start."

"Well, I'm not going to be here, so I sure hope someone can fill in for me," I said. "Your parents seem to be used to the idea."

Nolan nodded and then looked over and waved at his parents. "Yeah, they actually watched a Braves game with me yesterday. And, we got a ping-pong table for our basement, so we have a sport the whole family can play."

I excused myself from the bleachers to help clean the dugout. I wanted as much time near the Piper Bell field as I could get. I was tossing out some crushed Gatorade cups when Rachel, the sixth grader from the talent squad, walked up.

"I voted for your boyfriend," she said. "I'm sorry he lost.

I heard a rumor that you're definitely moving. Is that true?"

"I think I am," I said, even though it was hard to say. "Unless something goes really wrong for my dad."

"Well, here's the thing. I joined the talent squad after we talked, and I like it, but what's been really cool is making so many friends. I didn't think it was possible when I started here," she said. "And I kind of owe you, because I wasn't going to join anything until you said it was a good idea."

"I'm glad you like the talent squad. Katy will help you find your talent. Or, do the yoga with Coach Raddock," I said. "It's really true if you clear your head, ideas pop up."

"No, I have a talent," Rachel said. "I want to do a podcast called *When Life Gives You Lemons*. It's sort of an advice show and I wanted to launch it in the new year. Would you . . . want to be on it with me? It doesn't really matter if you're in Seattle. It's almost cooler if you are! I mean, not for you but . . . ."

"I get it," I told her, as my phone buzzed with Katy, Johnny, and Diego asking me to go out for my Last Post-Game Celebration. This time, I didn't mind so much.

"And, it might be fun to do it." I thought of you, Playbook. Maybe I'd even tell the world about you. "I'm in."

TO THE NINTH (INNING) DEGREE

Goal: Find a way to get extra innings in Peach Tree
Action: Be on the lookout for signs from the universe

Post-Day Analysis:
October 2

I was walking home from Diego's just now. We were doing homework together, acting like we'd be doing homework together for the rest of our lives, which we knew we wouldn't be, which was maybe why we were trying so hard to pretend like everything was totally normal. But I'd told him about Seattle being pretty much for sure, and he'd said, "Oh." And then we started scratching things down on our homework and muttering to ourselves about that homework.

It was the kind of nice silence you could only have with someone you'd known your whole life, but then Diego stopped scribbling to ask: "So . . . you don't think there's going to be a bloop and a blast?"

It was a saying invented by one of his favorite sportscasters, Bob Prince, who'd announced for the Pirates a long time ago. (He was most famous for saying, "Kiss it goodbye!" when someone got a home run.)

OTHER GUNNERISMS (SAYINGS OF BOB PRINCE, SPORTSCASTER KNOWN AS THE GUNNER)

- Aspirin tablets (when a fastball was going so fast it looked as tiny and hard to hit as an aspirin would be)

- Atem balls (a line drive to an infielder—it was going right at 'em)

- How sweet it is! (a Pirates victory, or a home run)

- Radio ball (a pitch the batter could hear but couldn't see)

- Mary Edgerley (no one knew who this was, but Prince ended every broadcast with, "Good night, Mary Edgerley, wherever you are.")

A bloop and a blast is sort of a last-minute game-changing play in baseball (sort of like when a football quarterback throws a crazy long pass—or a Hail Mary—to score when there seems to be no chance). The bloop is a batter hitting a single and the blast is the next batter getting a home run, and you really want to get a blast to follow a bloop if your team is down by one point in the ninth inning.

"The last game was yesterday," I said, sort of confused by his question. Diego had been at the game. "Piper Bell finished third overall, remember?"

"No, I mean for you, and Seattle," he said. "I guess . . . do you think your parents will change their minds?"

I shook my head. "I think my dad really wants to go."

"There's no chance that something might change?"

"There's a tiny possibility it won't work out," I said. "But he was on the phone with someone from the paper this morning, so I think it's going to happen."

But just now, as I was walking to my house and looking at the sky—and swinging my arms, both of them!!—I could have sworn the clouds looked a little like me and my Dad and Peter and Louie.

Maybe I'm seeing things because I've been thinking about our family so much and staying here, or moving. But there we were: Cloud Garcias. Here. In Peach Tree. Not in Seattle.

CLOUDS IN THE SHAPE OF MY FAMILY (MUST BE A GOOD SIGN)

You could accept a thing was happening and still want a different thing to happen, right?

And what I wanted was everything to align so that staying in Peach Tree was the best thing for everyone. I wanted a bloop and a blast that sealed the win and made us all happy. But that would have been a miracle.

When I rounded the corner for home, Peter was sitting on the porch with an envelope. A thick yellow envelope. "What took you so long?" he asked me.

"I didn't know you were waiting for me!"

He rolled his eyes, then waved the envelope around. "It's from the **COMMITTEE**."

So a committee could be for anything, but I knew right away what he meant. **THE COMMITTEE** was the deciding force for the Community Alliance Peach Tree Citizen of the Year Award. And committees didn't use giant envelopes if all that was inside was a letter that they didn't pick you.

"Whoa! Is this the bloop or the blast?" I said out loud.

"A blob or a what?" Peter said, but he didn't wait for an answer because he was already ripping open the envelope.

Inside was exactly what I hoped would be inside: my dad was the Peach Tree Citizen of the Year!

"We have to tell him," I said, "**NOW**!"

Peter ran into the house ahead of me, which under many circumstances would have bugged me, but today I let it slide. Peter had been my teammate on the All-Pros Play from day one. What if entering Dad for the award had been the bloop and winning was the blast and Peach Tree got to keep the REAL Garcias and not the cloud ones?

Dad was sitting at the kitchen table, which was weird. He has a problem with sitting. It's half the reason why deadlines can be extra-tough on him. Keeping his butt in a chair—a writing essential—is like asking me not to be great at baseball. Almost impossible.

Peter and I trampled in as Peter pushed the packet across the table at Dad.

"Wow, synchronized stomping. Should I be nervous?"

"Just read it!" I said, and as Dad pulled the papers toward him, I saw him notice the fancy stationery and the first lines of the letter.

"What did you guys do?" Dad asked, but he was smiling. "You entered me? Together?"

We nodded like a set of eager puppy dogs.

"Wow," he said. "Well . . . hmm. I don't know what to say." He looked teary. "Thank you."

I waited, for what, I didn't know, and then Dad said, "And, well, I need to talk to you both. But separately."

Peter and I exchanged a look and it was like my long-time dream to be able to read thoughts had finally come true. I knew we were thinking the same thing.

I went first. Dad suggested we talk at the park. *Our* park. After the clouds and the letter, I thought maybe he'd tell me that the whole idea of Seattle had been a huge mistake. That he couldn't leave behind all these memories. I mean, we were headed to the park down the street, where I'd had my thirteenth birthday party but also where I'd spent a million summer nights with Dad, just playing catch. Where Dad had told me he was marrying Louie. Where Dad later taught me to throw faster and harder. Where he told me not to be nervous the night before the first day I pitched on my Little League team.

Like my tree, it was a big deal, our park.

"Catch?" he said and held up a ball. He tossed me my mitt and I put it on, and I couldn't believe I hadn't gotten home from getting my cast off and done that immediately. My mitt felt like home. Dad tossed a throw lightly at me and I plucked it out of the sky. It didn't hurt to catch the ball, but it felt weird, the way putting on long pants after a summer of wearing shorts could feel weird.

"You okay?" Dad pointed at my arm.

"Yep," I said, talking only about my arm. Dad was talking about more than my arm.

"You know you and your brother are loons, right?" Dad said, catching my throw. "The best loons I know, but still loons."

"It's Peach Tree that picked you as Citizen of the Year. We just suggested it," I said.

"Well, I appreciate it," he said. "And everything you two did."

Did. Past tense. What did it mean?

We tossed the ball back and forth a bunch more, in that same kind of silence I had with Diego. I like it sometimes, having quiet, because, Playbook, you might have noticed my brain can be kind of loud. Even when it's quiet, it sometimes still has conversations.

Bob: *This is nice.*

Judy: *It is. But is it TOO nice?*

Bob: *Why do you have to ruin it, Judy?*

"I know I wasn't too happy with that application to the *Atlanta Herald*, but I am impressed with how you're pushing to stay in Peach Tree," Dad said.

I thought of a million questions, but I didn't ask any of them. I caught his throws and waited. It was hard not to talk when I really wanted to.

"Your mom was like that," Dad said. **EMOTIONAL CURVEBALL ALERT!** "Loyal. When she loved something, she'd dig in her heels and hold on for dear life. I can be flighty, but she was always sure."

He held the ball in the air, about to throw back to me, but then put his arm down. "I should have told you before

we even took the Seattle trip what I was thinking about," he said. "It wasn't fair."

I knew, right then, Playbook, that he was going to say he took the job. Part of me wanted clouds to roll over the sun and the world to get gloomy and rain to fall—whatever ominous (seriously, I'm learning so many good words. Piper Bell is quite a school!) signs it took for Dad to think that what he had to say next was all wrong. But part of me was okay when it stayed sunny and calm as Dad said, "But I got the job." He held the ball in midair, waiting for my reaction. "I know you aren't happy about it, but I hope you'll give Seattle a chance."

"So you're going to be a sportswriter for a major newspaper?" I said, instead of the million other things in my head. "Like you've always wanted?"

"It looks that way," he said. "I wish I didn't have to disappoint you and Peter to do it."

I'm not disappointed, though. I'm nervous. I'm sad. I wish I could be in two places at once. But I guess I'm a little excited for a whole new adventure. And, face it, if I make it to the majors, I'll probably have to move at least once as a key player who's sought after by many teams. Plus away games, and maybe even a season in Japan. I've always thought it would be cool to play in Japan.

I knew for sure at least one person who'd back me through whatever.

I ran to my dad and gave him a huge hug.

Leaving was going to be a tough play to handle. But sometimes getting through the tough stuff is part of being on a great team.

VICTORY LAP (SORT OF)

The Community Alliance Award Banquet was a big deal.
OR it was going to be. It was being held at the Town Hall,
in the Rotunda, this round room at the top of the building
where, on a clear day, you could see all the way to the next
town. At night, it was bound to look beautiful.

For the moment, I'm packing. We leave in a few weeks
and, well, Seattle might be okay. For one, my new school's
spring break is in early March, and Dad and Louie said
we'll come back here for a visit. And then, in April, Diego
and the Parker family will come to see us!

I'm still nervous, and I already know there are going to
be days when I'm really miserable about the move. But I
guess it would be kind of weird to have a baseball season
where you know you're going to win every game ahead
of time. What would be the point? So maybe life is like

that, too, and you can't know when your wins are going to come.

Plus, I have you, Playbook. And the me that goes into coming up with plays. As teammates go, I'm pretty good to have on my side.

(Little brother intrusion pause.)

Did I mention Peter's back to barging in my room? It's annoying. But also, familiar in a way I can rely on. Annoyingly familiar is about the right way to describe the new new Peter. Who, by the way, caught a glimpse of you, Playbook.

"I knew it!" he said. "You're making plans again!"

I shook my head and closed you, Playbook. I didn't toss you under anything this time. "I'm between plays right now."

I'd prepared for this moment. Or, well, a different moment than one where Peter walked in like he owned my room, but it was as good a time as any. I took out a notebook just like this one, Playbook, but on the inside cover I'd written "Peter Garcia's Playbook."

Peter looked down at it and flipped through the pages, which were blank, of course. He has to decide how he's going to approach his plays on his own.

"Is this for me?"

"It has your name on it."

"So you just, like, write about life and stuff?"

"There's a strategy," I said. "I'll help you, if you want."

He nodded. "Thanks."

PETER'S
VERY OWN
PLAYBOOK

PETER GARCIA'S
PLAYBOOK

He looked around my room at the spaces where my posters used to be. "You're gonna hang up your Mo'Ne Davis poster in our new house, right?"

I nodded. "Definitely."

"Then it's not like everything will be **TOTALLY** different," he said.

"We're probably still going to have rooms next to each other," I said. "And you'll probably still bug me all the time."

"Promise," Peter said.

It was good to have that to count on.

"Kids, it's almost time to go!" Louie hollered up the stairs.

Almost time to go. To the banquet, and later, Seattle. There was no way to know what to expect, except that my family would be there.

I don't exactly have a play in mind, but at least I know who's on my team.

ACKNOWLEDGMENTS

In the course of writing the Gabby Garcia's Ultimate Play-book series, I've had the chance to think about and answer the question, "When did you know you wanted to be a writer?" And I always say I started late at writing fiction, that I didn't know writing books was something that any book- and word-loving person could try her hand at, that it took me a while to realize that, while getting a book pub-lished was hard, writing a book was entirely something I could do.

But, if I think on it longer, I might amend that. I think I knew I wanted to write books very early, at least since I first insisted on bringing a pile of books on a long road trip and almost looked forward more to the time in the car with the books than the destination itself. Or since the time I had to call my mom to come pick me up from the library after I'd planned on walking home, because I couldn't carry the thir-ty-one books I'd checked out. Or when I read a book by a particular author (and there've been a few) and then wanted to read every word that person had ever written. (I still do all these things, but what I'm trying to say is that my passion for reading should have tipped me off that I wanted to be a writer.)

So, now, as I think about who I want to thank—and saying thank you is a lucky thing, I think—I don't know where to start. There are infinite possibilities and a limited word count. But over the years there've been family members, librarians, teachers, friends, random people who said funny things in conversation at the supermarket checkout line, people who paid in exact change at the greeting card shop where I worked, and had such a particular way about them, I never forgot their mannerism . . . you get the idea. I've been fortunate to be in this life game with so many people who've in countless ways big and small been influential, and who've all made a difference in who I am and what I write. And there've been books. Can I first and foremost thank books and the people who write them, and edit them, and illustrate them, and make them? Because books always have and always will be treasured friends to me, and I hope they are to you, too, reader.

Okay, as to this one in your hands, I will be more specific. For seeing the potential in Gabby from well before she stepped up to the plate, I'd like to thank Claudia Gabel, and for coaching Gabby all the way to the last inning, Stephanie Guerdan. And thank you to Katherine Tegen and her entire team for allowing me the privilege and opportunity to share this character and her stories. The team of Emily Rader, Mitchell Thorpe, and Emma Meyer ensure that these books get out into the world and that people might hear about them, and for all of their efforts, I am grateful. For bringing the spirit of Gabby to every last element of this book, from cover to cover and every page in between, a mega thanks to the design team of David Dewitt, Amy Ryan, and Katie Fitch.

I'd never written books with illustrations before the Gabby series, and I feel so lucky that Gabby brought Marta Kissi into my life. It's always a treasure when you feel like someone can translate the oddball images that pop into your head and make them a million times better than your brain even imagined. Marta, someday we'll meet in person, whether in London or L.A.!

I heap gratitude upon Fonda Snyder for offering support and advice and a cheering section, too.

This Gabby in particular is about family, and I couldn't write without mine. It starts with my mom and dad, Bill and Debra Palmer, who provided inspiration from day one, often by sharing the things they love with me. From my dad's love of baseball, so devoted that I recall once making a bat and ball from a stick and a pinecone on a long road trip, to my mom's love of cooking and—up until the day she died—trying out new recipes or developing her own; you'll see their marks on all the Gabby books, and on me. (They also passed on a love of reading and of books.)

Gabby's brother, Peter, figured more prominently in this book and although Gabby took a while to realize her brother could also be a friend, I've been lucky enough to feel that way about my brother, Bill, from day one. We grew up sharing favorite movies and books (even if our tastes didn't always intersect) and we're still lucky enough to be having conversations about them to this day, and many others.

When you have kids, people sometimes ask how you manage to write with them, but when it comes to my sons Clark and Nate, I can't imagine writing without them. (And not just because they both peer over my shoulder from time to time asking how many pages I wrote and how big the book will be and and and. . . .) They are both more responsible for my creativity than I can ever explain, for the questions they ask, the love they share, and the selves they're becoming. I'm inspired by them both and proud of them in ways beyond measure.

There's always more to say than can possibly be articulated about my husband, Steve, who has never doubted me and reminds me often to not doubt myself. I am not always easy to live with, especially in the middle of writing a book, and he takes it in stride when I interrupt a conversation with some urgent book thought that pops into my head and needs immediate feedback, or when I encounter a case of the yips. He never fails to cheer me up when I'm in a slump but just as important, he is there to celebrate the wins, too. Like only the best of the best teammates do, he comes through, time and again. If I mention that he's smart, funny, and good-looking, it will sound like I'm bragging, and I am.

And, finally, whether this is the first Gabby book you've read or if you've been with Gabby from book one, I want to thank you, the reader. Books can exist without readers, but you give them their real lives and this author is grateful.